Leviathan Rising

ANN TRACY

anntracy@charter.net

518 563-4066

12 Addoms St., Plattsburgh, NY 12901

DECORATION DAY FOR THE WOMEN

Brenna, my mother

Geneva, my aunt

Susie and Louisa, my grandmothers

Eileen, my mentor

CONTENTS

ACKNOWLEDGEMENTS

First, to Earl Hoffmann, who gave me Odin, name and all, and his Voyage and the Beast. From this sprang also Athena and Junior, the obsession with catching Leviathan, the particulars of Joab's end, and the chapter on bait. Further, there was collusion on the rapture of metal.

Friends let me read to them—Lisa Lewis, Sally Sears Mack, the Rev. Teri Monica, Jenni Pickard, and Sylvia Stack, as well as the aforementioned Earl and his mother Greta. Also Vera Vivante, Doug Skopp, Laura Palkovic, Cynthia Newgarden, and Jan Maher, who were more or less captive. Others read the thing from end to end (some of them, heroically, an earlier draft)—Pat Hoffmann, Alexis Levitin, Mary Jane Miranda, Dorothy and Brian Parker, Pam Taylor, Barbara McGillicuddy—and made useful remarks, most memorably Pat's observation that I had not put in any dogs. I owe Alexis Levitin, always, for his general savvy advice. And finally to Virginia Cantarella for formatting the book and doing the illustrations, including the cover.

CHAPTER ONE

Come afternoon recess it was pouring buckets. The shortest legs, hanging from the seats and touching nothing, would ache by now, needing to stretch and run. The big boys would be restless in spirit, needing a break from classroom manners. The room seethed with distress; Lille, teacher at twenty-two, could feel it and pity it. Indeed she shared it: not only did she have a maddening itch on her left calf and two loose hairpins, she wanted to run in the rain and she couldn't. Eighteen faces turned to her for hope.

"Outhouse for those who need it," she said, "and we can all thank the School Committee for that covered walkway. Youngest class first--nobody fall through, now!--oldest class last. Girls may go in pairs. Boys one at a time, it's not a place to play. *It's not a place to shove your brother's head down the hole,* she meant, having seen some of that in her first year or two teaching a one-room school.

"Well then," she said, when they were all accounted for again. "Another chapter of *Treasure Island*? Or would you rather sing?"

"No, tell about Leviathan," said Gladys, whose face needed washing, and added "please, Miss Lille Nickerson." That child had never had any show at home-- her mother took fits and fell on the floor, and everyone said her father'd let them all starve before he'd turn a hand's work--but Gladys could read now and appeared to be getting a taste for geography. Her suggestion, though not original, was popular, and feeling herself approved of, she smiled widely, showing her new second molars, good as anybody's.

"Well, then, Ladies and Gentlemen," Lille said, "Citizens of Leviathan, Maine, how do you suppose our town, our municipality, got its name?"

Millie Goss, pale as cottage cheese, who'd got herself saved at last summer's revival and never let anyone forget it, leaped in first. "It's in the BIBLE," she said with a showy disdain for the hell-bound. "God made a giant big fish called Leviathan to play in the giant big ocean, Psalm 104."

"And does anyone see a joke in that? Irony?" said Lille. "Big fish, small town?"

"Not small!" cried Harold Smith, shocked, himself the scrawnier of twins. "Got a baseball field!" He was six.

His twin Hugh, much the smarter one, patted his back. They shared a fold-down seat. "Not as big as Houlton, she means," he explained kindly. "Or Danforth."

"Some people," Lille said it like a song they knew, "think Leviathan was named in hopes that the name would make our town grow big, very big, enormous. There are towns in Maine called after whole countries, you know—China, Norway-- but those towns are quite small. What does this teach us, Children?"

"Doesn't work," growled one of the big boys. Lille was pleased. He had weighed cause and effect.

"And other people," she said, "think that a pretty good-sized fish was caught here in East Grand Lake about the time the town was named. And of course you don't want to name a town 'Pretty Good-sized Fish,' do you." Laughter.

"And," she said finally, arriving where all her audience had been waiting, "of course some people say that there's a giant aquatic creature living in the lake, also called Leviathan."

"Don't you believe in our lake monster?" one of the medium-sized boys asked, anxious.

"My father says it's there," Gladys cried, "he says he's seen it, but he might have been drunk." Howls of approving laughter. Lille knew that a proper teacher would say, "Oh, I'm sure he wasn't," but she was pretty sure he was, and she didn't like to lie. Besides, Gladys had scored twice in one day, it would be mean to spoil it.

"And he says he'll catch it too!" Gladys went on.

Not if it takes any work, Lille thought, and turned to the anxious boy. How to be true and yet not spoil his faith? "I believe in as many things as I can," she said, "because believing makes the world a more exciting place, doesn't it. I believe in Jo March and the boys in our last book, in one way. They're real in our minds when we read it. I believe in a different way that tadpoles turn into frogs: you wouldn't expect it, but we've seen it. I won't know which way I believe in the lake monster unless I see him. Or her. Which I hope I do."

"Odin Crocker has seen him," said the boy, insistent.

"No," said Frank Putnam, a confident sixth-grader who was tough enough to be widely trusted. "Odin Crocker saw a sea serpent when he was a cabin boy; that was in the ocean. That was different. I've heard him tell about it."

"What about God then, Miss Nickerson? Which Leviathan did he make?" That was Millie Goss of course, damn the girl anyway. Lille heard tales of teachers who'd lost their jobs from answering a God question wrong, though never, as far as she knew, in Leviathan, where replacements were scarce.

"Ah, God," said Lille, "our Creator, in whom we live and move and have our being! What a big question, Millie. We can talk about that further when the minister comes for Bible lessons next week. But now let's talk a little more about the monster some of you think might be in our lake. How big, do you imagine? And what color?" Hands shot up. Rumors and testimonies flew. All of them apparently believed in Leviathan, not "some."

In mid-afternoon, rain over and children off the leash, Lille took the short way home through the town graveyard. The grass was mowed there, some chance she could keep her skirts dry, while the roads would be pure mud (once so lovely to wade in barefoot that she still longed for the silk of it between her toes). Walking past familiar stones, the names like titles of books too late to read though she knew the stories, she pitied the generation of the last war, dead too young, or old now, whiskery and hitching, the women widowed or bereaved in girlhood of husbands that might have been. "Civil," *my suffering rear-end!* she thought. Evil luck to be born twenty years or so before a war. Or less, even--here was the grave of Isaiah Ledbetter, sixteen, sold as a substitute by his wretch of a father, who'd claimed the boy was nineteen, a scandal still. Isaiah's story hurt her. Making sure nobody saw her silliness, she dropped a piece of biscuit on his grave. She guessed that on top of everything else, he'd have died pretty hungry.

Her brother Liberty was coming up the rise to meet her, which might mean he had news or might mean he'd burned out on barn chores and left the rest to the hired man. Someday it might be bad news about their mother, but not yet.

"Fall in the mud, Lib?" she asked.

"Bejeezely black-hearted son of a goddam pig knocked me over and rolled me!" he said

"Millie Goss would say you'll never go to heaven talking that way," she said.

"Don't want to," said Lib, "if there's pigs there. Horses and cows don't like me much, and that pig outright hates me, so if things with four hooves go to heaven, hell will suit me first rate."

"That pig is the one bound for hell, don't you worry," she said. "Would have got the hired man the other day if he hadn't climbed a fence. I guess we won't cry too much when we butcher him. Barn cats catch anything today? And how's the skunk? You'd have told me right off if Mother was any worse, wouldn't you?"

"Barn cats are doing fine. Ace brought Mother a mouse's head for a treat, got her laughing. I don't know but what she's some better today. Seems a little perked up. She asked for MacDuff too, she does love that skunk, so I picked him up and dropped him on her bed. They went right nose to nose. Hired girl isn't easy with him yet, but he never sprayed anybody, I tell her--one of the family, the old cat raised him."

"I believe you're sweet on that nice, fat hired girl, Lib," she teased.

"Her!" said Lib.

Teasing, they'd pair each other up with people who'd be a good deal worse than the hired girl, worse indeed than nobody, mindful even while they joked that nobody might be who they'd wind up with. That like many another pair of siblings they might find themselves growing old together in the home place, left-overs from the mating years. That would be no laughing matter, but still they bantered on.

Lille reckoned that at least she knew how love felt, though nobody else would think her experiences counted. At four, the age of idolatry, she had worshipped her Sunday School teacher-- her honey-colored hair, the sweet tones of her voice. They sang, "When He cometh, when He cometh, to make up his jewels," and Lille, gazing up at the red sealing-wax beads strung around her teacher's smooth neck, supposed that they were those very jewels, the bright gems for His throne. Mary, the Biblical sister who'd chosen the better part, wore her teacher's face; so did Rachel, worth fourteen years' labor. She was the heroine of all stories. Once she'd wiped Lille's nose with her own handkerchief and told her keep it, which until Lille reconsidered it some years later seemed romantic.

At twelve, needing a hero, Lille had worked up a passion for President Benjamin Harrison, who was honoring Maine that summer with a leisurely visit to Mount Desert Island. She cut his picture out of the paper and put it in the drawer under her aprons, nearly persuaded that she cared for politics but in the end too honest not to see that she fancied the cut of his bushy white beard more than his innovations. All the same he gave her an interest that summer, when she needed one. Her father, making note of her reading, reminded her that she'd never be president, she'd have to settle for First Lady. She thought she could enjoy that, thank you, though she had her own ideas about the rise of women.

At sixteen she had a scholarship to Coburn, a boarding school a hundred miles or so downstate, and one weekend she went home with her roommate, who promised her a look at Mount Desert Island, a trade-off for Lille's whispered account, after lights-out one night, of her former passion for President Harrison. Their snorts and giggles had earned them demerits, but not many; the teacher on duty had a sense of humor too. Lille had loved it at Coburn, and she loved the promised view of ocean from the top of Cadillac Mountain, but more yet had she loved her roommate's brother, who flirted and played with her while he packed for California, where he stayed. She and her roommate corresponded, so she sometimes had news of him. Now and then, knowing it impossible, Lille fantasized stepping off a train into his tanned and muscled Californian arms, after which climactic moment she'd never again have any truck with hairpins or corsets.

In truth she only wore the appearance of corsets now, having slipped out the bones and hidden them under her mattress, which seemed to her a fair compromise between expectation and self- will.

Lib hadn't gone to high school. He'd been a dreamy boy without much academic grip, glad to be released to planting and harvesting, and thus he'd missed the temptation of female classmates in their first awakening. His desire, rather, was fixed on nature, the land and the lake. He was fond of his neighbors, both domestic and wild, both footed and pawed, but his real love was the water and the boat in which he idled on it.

In winter Lib kept that rowboat in the Currans' boathouse. Like other Houlton folks—like folks as far as Bangor too, who came north on the train—the Curran family had a summer camp on the edge of the lake, comfortable, not at all snooty but interesting. They'd offered him the boathouse space and he was glad to use it. Kept an eye out for their place as a payback. Curran was a lawyer; she was a high school teacher, or had been till they married. Story was his father was dead and he was the oldest, so he couldn't get away to high school until he was most twenty, and there he was all of a sudden in her English class, big, handsome young man, and she was tiny, brisk, and single. There were jokes from the idlers on the steps of the store about how the Currans managed in the bedroom, but it was none of his business; they were smart people and treated him nice, and he reckoned they'd have worked something out if one of them had been a colt and the other a pickerel. They had a daughter, Eileen, big-boned like her dad and smart as a chipmunk but wouldn't talk till she was four. Just didn't care to. Proved how smart she was, to his mind, but it had worried her folks some. She was around six now and talked plenty. Lib liked her.

He'd take and row his boat down along the shore until he got to the Thoroughfare, and the water would pat the flat bottom of it like a welcome. Then it was under the bridge, head for North Lake, and next thing he knew he was up Monument Stream, where all was freedom and peace. Winters he'd sit by the kitchen stove and whittle out some animals, often ones he'd see on the shores of Monument or in the water; that soothed his mind too. He'd made a whole beaver family for the Currans' little girl last winter. Hadn't seen her yet to give it to her. He'd made a coon for old Odin Crocker's wife Athena, next house down from Lille and Lib's. Athena and Odin had a smart coon (smarter than Odin, the neighbors said) that wintered inside and would hide under the sink **if he** didn't like the looks of a dropper-in or if Odin got going on about that one trip of his as a cabin boy when he'd lived down on the coast: "On my voyage," he'd begin, "I saw the Serpent, the Beast of the Waters," and about the time he said "voyage" the raccoon would strike for the pantry or the cellar, whichever was nearest. Athena herself told that tale.

Haney Brook Road was a friendly place for wild things, Lib thought—their skunk, the Crockers' raccoon, and Susie and Perley Junkins had a rabbit that beat all. Perley used to claim they were teaching it to read. He'd have to whittle them a rabbit with a book next winter, they'd like that. "Leviathan is just a narrow place on the map," Susie had told Lib one time when he was about ten, "but it seems wider when you know the other species socially."

CHAPTER TWO

On fine afternoons, now that the woodstove in the general store was cold and Decoration Day on the calendar, the slackers who'd sat inside and talked all winter moved out to sit on the front steps, which were long as bleachers and commanded a view of the baseball field, the lake, and a small but moving pageant on which to comment— shoppers, schoolchildren, strangers on the way to Houlton, Joab Nutter the minister and his edgy wife. Odin was a regular on the steps, along with Ruby Wayne, the useless father of Gladys, a man who when his wife had a fit would so often kick her and say, "You cut that out, Edna Mabel!" that it had grown to be a kind of byword. There'd be a Civil War vet or so who'd come home short a limb, any guy who came to buy a harrow tooth and felt too lazy to go home and install it, and pretty often some respectable joker like Perley to tease them. Two or three dogs. Lib never sat, though he acted friendly enough. You had to, everyone was a neighbor. The feel of the talk put him off. He didn't think he liked 1899, a year too near the edge and squirmy as a pocket full of fishing worms.

The ones bold enough to skip church sat on the steps Sunday mornings too, and nobody spoke a disapproving word to them in public on account of the vets with their missing bits, which is not to say that Athena didn't work Odin over when she got him home. An old maid or two had tried to stir up the selectmen to interfere, but in vain. The store was closed, there was a CLOSED ON SUNDAY sign right on the door, and if the weather got bad the storekeeper would come out and let them in the back door, purely social and who could say it wasn't, when he lived over the store. The dogs went home, or pretended to. And if somebody picked up some crackers and somebody else cut a wedge of rat cheese and they shared them around and left some coins on the counter, the store was still shut, it was nobody's business.

It was looking to rain now but it hadn't spit yet. The idlers gazed at the clouds, holding out their palms to catch warning drops, and went on arguing about Leviathan, the one in the lake. Or not.

"He's out there, dammit," said Odin. "On my Voyage I saw his brother the Great Beast."

"Suppose he is," said the vet with the peg leg, "what you going to do about it."

Lib and Lille were regular church-goers, not so much for piety as for a number of other motives. Habit was one. Their family had always gone, and staying away would cause more stir than it was worth, particularly since Lille was the schoolteacher, though that wouldn't have brought her out on a Sunday if she had any conviction to the contrary. Also, it was a gathering with the possibility of observing a new outfit, a new couple, an unseemly outburst. It was even a kind of theatrical entertainment if the minister was either pretty good or pretty bad. Their mother, not yet well enough to get there herself, liked to hear what she'd missed.

It began to thunder in the middle of the sermon, but not enough to drown out Joab Nutter's oratory. He paced the platform as he spoke, giving the pulpit a slap for emphasis whenever he passed it. His coat flapped behind him, a kind of antique coat with tails shaped like a beatle's butt, and greenish with age. For three Sundays already he'd preached about the Last Days, and his diagram of those horrors, pasted to a plank, leaned against the choir loft behind him. Seven seals, seven candlesticks, and the pregnant women scrambling for the hills to escape the beasts like scorpions. Lille hadn't been listening hard. She did like the four thundering horsemen of the Apocalypse, though, especially the part when Nutter had got so wound up he tossed his mane and whinnied.

Now and then, too, he burst into ecstatic song, his wild hair in his eyes, and the children squirmed against their giggles, elbowed by their parents. Lille thought that if she had a child, or had had the foresight to borrow one, she might have pretended it needed to pee and taken it out. She couldn't cheat her mother out of the funny parts, though. On Sundays the Nickersons gave themselves two treats-- chocolate cake and a reprise of Nutter's latest performance.

"Thief in the night! Jesus comes as a thief in the night!" cried Joab Nutter as the thunder rolled. "You don't see a thief when he creeps into your house to take away the things you love. What do you value most?"

"Fishing pole!" answered a child who didn't know about rhetorical questions.

"Doll stove!" whispered a toddler with a ruffle around the neck of her dress.

"Mama!" sobbed an astute child who could see where this might be going, and a whole row broke down into howls. Jesus would kidnap their *mamas*?

The minister looked at the grieving children with cold satisfaction. He could use their tears. Lille and Lib exchanged a glance. They had never hated him more. This was beyond funny.

"That's right, Little Ones," he said, leaning forward from the pulpit where he had briefly come to rest. "You can laugh and play now, but the book of Matthew in the Holy Bible, the Bible that perhaps sits on your parlor table unread, says that two will be together at the End and one of them will be taken, one left behind. Two will be in the field digging potatoes, and one will rise into the sky with potatoes still earthen in his hand. And the other, the one who was not God's chosen, the one who had not followed his commandments and been his faithful servant, will be left sitting in the dirt gazing into the heavens, into Heaven where he'll never come, and weeping with despair, for he'll know in that moment that it's all true, every word that I'm saying is true. And two will be sleeping together in a bed, yes, two little children perhaps, and one will have a bad dream that wakens him, but when he reaches out his brother is gone. He gets out of bed and in his bare feet searches for his companion, but he can't be found. The house is empty—parents gone, grandma gone, the hired man gone out of the shed chamber, for those were all in God's grace, God loved them because they did his will, but the child left behind was a scoffer and a heathen and a Sabbath breaker who will see the terrible horsemen of the apocalypse and know the wrath of the scorpion. Yea truly the Lake Monster Leviathan may rise up to heaven, if he's honored God, but the man weeping on his knees in the half-dug field of potatoes has missed his chance. Watch, I say, be ready. The Lord will come as a thief in the night, when you least expect him."

Demoralized children and not a few adults were sobbing by then, and still the thunder cracked. There'd be some sleepless households that night, Lille reckoned, and some vacancies in her school tomorrow. Oblivious, clearly enjoying himself, Nutter burst once again into narcissistic song, waving his arms: "When the Roll is called up yonder, when the Roll is called up yonder, when the Roll is called up yon-DER, when the Roll is called up yonder I'll be there!" He emphasized the pronoun. The pianist caught up for part of it.

"Well, Joab, I guess we can spare you if you'd like to go now," Lib whispered under the last triumphant chord, and Lille felt her diaphragm jog with suppressed laughter. She whacked his foot with the side of hers. She was the teacher, she mustn't snort. Not with all the weeping. "But there is reason to be happy," said Nutter, settling his hair with the palms of his hands, "there is reason to rejoice, not only for what we will gain but for what we will avoid, what even those terrified, left and bereft, facing the scorpions, may avoid. God will not make us endure a new century, or not for long. You may have seen certain cartoons, drawings of a world of strange vehicles that eschew our friends the horses, a world where women wear short skirts, displaying their nether limbs, and lounge with cigarettes in their wicked fingers, unsexing themselves; where men fly through the sky like great effeminate birds in stockings and boots. An unfamiliar and utterly uncongenial world!"

Count me in! Bring it on! thought Lille. The bliss of cutting that pile of hair! No more hairpins skating down her back like bugs. Light skirts, short skirts, even trousers like Lib's, the freedom of it! She wanted it worse than the vote, though for justice she wanted that too. She was not yet twenty-five, she might have fifty years of a new world where humans took to the air and she took to her heels. For the first time in that church she prayed with fervor: *Let me grow old, Lord, let me be free! If you love me, don't swoop me up yet. Show me the twentieth century. Let me see my brother fly.*

It being Sunday, they turned right and walked past the baseball field and the general store. Home the long way, by the roads. There had been less rain than thunder, just enough to lay the dust.

"I see all them little ones come out blatting, and some of the old folks too," said the one-armed veteran leaning on the store front. "Pretty tough sermon?"

"Believe it," said Lille. "You missed some show."

"Guess I'll come along with you folks," said Perley, "since you're going past my house. You might stop and catch Susie up, Lille, she hurt her ankle hunting eggs in the haymow yesterday."

"I'll go along and tell Mother you're coming," Lib said. "Take your time."

"Thanks," Lille said. "Don't tell about the sermon and all the hoorah till I get there."

"Since when," said Lib, "have I been a talker?"

Perley laughed. "Since never."

Susie Jenkins was perhaps the best natured woman in all of Aroostook County. Crazy women who spoke to nobody else spoke to Susie. Ruby Wayne, who kicked his epileptic wife, raised his hat to Susie. There were cookies in her pantry, there was fresh bread and homemade jam and sweet butter. Susie put on the teakettle and

—

16

listened and laughed. Perley laughed too, at her and with her, about the neighbors and about the rabbit. They had one daughter, she lived down Bangor way, not so far if you took the train down from Houlton. "Lille!" Susie cried, "Come right in and put the kettle on. I'm keeping my ankle up! Now tell me what that damn fool of a minister's up to , and how your school's going. Do you mind the rabbit on the table? Perley made hot biscuits, and he's as good as I am. And that rabbit's crazy for Perley's biscuits, always wants more, you remember that's how come we called him Oliver Twist."

Lille gave Oliver a kind look and he took a hop nearer. He'd seen her before but not up close, not face to face. The biscuits weren't on the table yet; there might be time for her to pet him first if she was so inclined. Reading the rabbits' shy desire, she drew her fingers along his side, and of that too he wanted more, Lille was glad of it: he was softer than cats, softer than blown dandelions.

"That godforsaken sonofabitch," said Perley, after they'd had biscuits all around and tea for the humans. "that lowlife sanctimonious skunk—oh sorry Lille, don't tell MacDuff I said that—scaring the kids that way. I'd like to hang him up by his you-know-whats! They cry pretty hard?"

"Harold Smith took it bad about reaching over after a nightmare and not finding Hugh because he's been raptured. I hadn't realized he relied on Hugh so much, he seems so independent, but I should have seen it. Hugh's the one with answers. That little whey faced Millie Goss just looked smug; she expects to be the first one up. Gladys Wayne had come by herself as usual and didn't seem too cut up by the prospect of her parents being snatched away. Susie, if they are, what say we make her a new dress for church? Ruby can't trade it off if he's raptured.

"The littlest ones cried the worst—well, they would, all that stuff about their missing parents—and some of the grownups bawled right along, but it looked like the ones from about 12 to 25 had some idea Nutter'd gone crazy, or always had been crazy, or maybe all ministers were. We should have seen today coming on with the whole end-time thing, I guess, but we didn't. I've always made fun of that man, but now I can hardly say his name and keep my biscuit down. I

17

believe he gets worse every week. I'd like to live in a place with more than one church someday, I swear to God I would. If I was in Houlton I'd be Unitarian Universalist one Sunday and Episcopalian the next and maybe at Easter I'd go see how the Catholics taste. I bet not a one of them ever carries on about being left behind in a potato field!" The bare names of those other churches on her tongue were more nourishing than a whole sermon from the unsavory Joab Nutter, she thought. His wife, too, had looked as though she'd rather be any place else.

By the time Lille turned into the Nickerson yard and wiped her shoes on the grass, Lib had his feet up and their mother was napping with MacDuff in her arms. Nobody appeared to be holding a grudge because she'd lingered. "Father brought some kindling by," Lib said.

"Good," said Lille. "I'll make the cake for when she wakes up. We can have that cold chicken for supper. Did you tell her anything?"

"Just that Joab got everybody all worked up but you'd tell it when you got home because you'd tell it funnier. She got out of bed this afternoon and polished the silver. Said it didn't take all that much energy. Susie sent her up a magazine earlier."

They looked at each other, thinking but not saying that there were worse shit piles than Leviathan after all.

CHAPTER THREE

Lille had thought it out overnight and had a note ready when she got to school. It was perhaps stronger on clarity than tact, but she thought that was about right.

"Would you mind dropping this off at the parsonage before you pump the water?" she asked the two big boys who were starting off with the school bucket. One of them held out his hand for the folded paper, his grin conspiratorial as a wink; and she smiled back, trying to swallow the width of her amusement. She'd talked to teachers who found the older boys difficult, but she relished their joking and cynicism, she loved them. The note, which she correctly assumed they were going to read on the way, said "Mr. Nutter, I think we'll skip the Bible class this week while the children are still upset from the Rapture sermon. I'm capable of answering their questions until we see fit to reconvene." Let him shove that up his self-righteous butt and sit on it.

Casting her eyes over the room for empty seats, she was pleased to find after all no more than usual. A couple missing out of eighteen didn't signify. Millie Goss wasn't there, all the better—probably home packing for the Rapture—and one of the big girls sometimes didn't come till afternoon on wash days. Lille took her pitch-pipe out of the desk drawer. "Suppose we sing 'Marching through Georgia,'" she said. Leviathan still had enough fierce old vets to keep that popular, and it never failed to perk up a schoolroom. When they were through and sitting down, cheeks a little rosier, she made her announcement.

"If you were in church on Sunday and happen to be worried about anything you heard, if you'd feel better if we talked about it, well, you're welcome to eat your lunches in here with me at noon today and talk about it for a while before you go out and run around. You don't have to, but you're welcome to."

"Will you tell us the truth, Miss Nickerson?" That was her bold new girl who'd moved from Linneus. She appeared to have an inquiring mind, and might be fun.

Lille smiled. "What do you think?" she said.

"YES!" shouted the roomful, laughing.

It was a proud moment. She wouldn't tell Mother and Lib, though, because in Leviathan the story would get around and it would sound even better from somebody else. She heard it in her head—"My boy tells me your girl got quite a vote of confidence from the scholars yesterday."

Seven anxious children, mixed sexes, on the young side, had stayed in, and for the first quarter hour they all talked at once, yipping and shouting, with a whiff of theological dissension: *Is, Isn't, Will, Won't, No such of a thing!* When they'd subsided a bit their questions sorted out.

"Please, Miss Lille, is it really in the Bible about Jesus being a thief?"

"No, no," said Lille, "not <u>being</u>! It just says he'll come back when you don't expect him, not that he'll steal your things. If I said you could sing sweet as a bird, it wouldn't mean you had feathers, would it? You can compare one single part of two things, without the other parts getting into it. Know what I mean?"

Hugh nodded. "If I say the moon is round as a ball it doesn't mean it bounces." At six he already understood analogy and gave a better example than she had. She wanted to hug him but didn't. She'd try him on some fifth-grade books.

"So we <u>don't</u> know that it will happen right off, Miss Nickerson?" That was a third-grade girl, already looking just a bit less pale. She furrowed the butter on her bread with the tip of her finger, which she put in her mouth. She might think about eating again.

"Indeed we don't!" said Lille. "The Bible itself says we won't know, so I can't imagine why Mr. Nutter imagines he does know. Let's say he just got excited. It happens. We'll try to overlook his silliness, won't we. And let me tell you something else—nothing like that will happen just because the 19th century is winding down. Why, once upon a time the first century turned into the—Harold?"

"Second?"

"Yes! And the ninth century turned into the—Gladys?"

"Tenth!"

"And the fourteenth?" It was a full chorus now.

"Fifteenth!"

"And how did we get into our nineteenth century?"

A careful pause.

"From the eighteenth," said Hugh. Six. Sometimes you got a gift.

"Excellent. And did the world end any of those times? NO, it did not. Here we all are. And what will come at the end of December when the Nineteenth is finished?"

"Santa Claus!" yelled a little one, and everyone howled with relief.

"AND the Twentieth Century," said Lille, still laughing, "and it will be ours then, for all the rest of our lives. We'll feel so lucky to have it, because our new century will be full of amazing things, fast things, bright things, funny things. Me, I can't wait! And one more thing I want to tell you: if the Rapture really had happened last night, every single one of you, every single one, would have flown off hand-in-hand with all the people you love. Not even one of you would have been stuck here alone. Because, first, all of you are fine people, fully qualified for Heaven. And second, Jesus wouldn't separate children from their families like that anyway: there is not one scrap of evidence in the Bible that He's mean, not one, and whatever Mr. Nutter says, that would be a rotten mean thing to do. So-- Jesus just would not do that, no matter what mistake to the contrary you might hear some minister make when he's got his mind somewhere else. Would. Not. Got it? You all happier now? Then grab your lunches and go get some air.

21

When the last joyous heels disappeared out the door she walked to the pail and raised a dipperful of water like a toast. "Sucks to you, preacher," she said. "Sic transit gloria mundi!

As for Joab, even as she spoke he was loitering for the first time on the general-store steps with his purchase in his hand. While their dinner was cooking he had been sent by his wife to fetch half a pound of brown sugar. Brown. She knew he preferred white. Her face had looked sharp as a hatchet, sour as old milk, during his Rapture sermon, which he still thought had been rather powerful. Obviously powerful. Had there not been weeping and gnashing of teeth? He fancied that the men on the steps looked friendlier than sometimes. In fact that was a little true. His sermon had stirred things up, been a kind of scandal. They almost wished they'd heard it. He did not think well of them, nor (he supposed) did God, who surely had not sent his Son to die for the likes of them. Ruby Wayne, lazy and brutal. Odin Crocker, a braggart and liar. Two old men whose names he'd not bothered to learn, who hadn't fought for the North hard enough if they'd paid nothing for the Preservation of **the Union** but a hand or a foot.

"Well, men," he said in a manner intended to be hearty if condescending, "will I be seeing you in church next Sunday?"

"Gonna preach another sermon to make the babies cry?" said the old veteran who'd lost his left hand. He scratched his crotch with his right as he spoke.

"If it will save their souls, I'll preach it," said Joab, shifting his sugar unconsciously to the other hand.

"If it makes a stir I might come," drawled Ruby. "Boring out here now'n again. My Gladys said it was pretty funny." Gladys had said nothing of the sort, though she'd stayed calm through the tumult. He just wanted to give the asshole minister a little boot toe.

"I shall expect you," said Joab with great dignity, "and I shall speak to you again." He went home humming "Dare to be a Daniel," lyrics by P. Bliss. Behind him Ruby's dog lifted a leg.

"When I was on my voyage," said Odin, "I saw many a strange beast—but none a damn sight stranger than that one."

Mrs. Nutter, Emmeline to her friends back in Portland, would have concurred. She could see by now that she had married a creature much stranger then she knew. It had seemed an adventure, a kind of joke, to marry a minister and trek off to a place where the maps were sectioned into numbered townships, a place where only a few settlements even had names. And might have been an adventure, too, if she'd ever been free to enjoy it. She might have laughed, if she'd had friends to laugh with. She knew now that women she could have liked, if there were any, would never come near her, yoked as she was with the unsavory and pompous Joab. She saw their derision when he preached. She would have been part of it, in her other life. No, she wouldn't have been there, in her other life. She'd have been in some decent church, with a minister in proper clothes and a sermon about real things, and when the congregation laughed it would have been from a joke, and when they cried it would have been at a funeral.

Not even in bed did she feel free to laugh or cry now. Joab would know she was awake. It was one thing to pray, and another to be ordered to your knees.

CHAPTER FOUR

"Lib," his mother said, "you're a good boy, always were, and a good man, and you whale away at work I know you hate, with farm animals that drive you crazy, and all the time you're longing to be on the lake in that boat. This looks to be the prettiest spring day yet, so you'd better grab it if the major chores are done. I'll be okay, for all the hired girl's off sick; I can get up some, I just tucker out easy. Out of practice. Stop at Odin and Athena's if you want to, it's on your way, and ask Athena if she'd care to come up and sit a spell. I expect she'd like to get shut of Odin and have a little hen talk. I'd ask Susie but I think she and Perley have driven up to Houlton to meet the train."

Lib was touched, though he'd wouldn't have said it. He didn't expect to get noticed, not like that. He'd come to think of himself as a boy who got left: left on the farm when Lille went away to board at Coburn Classical; left to carry a man's burden when his father took off, dog and all; left with that terrible shovel to fill in the grave when his little sister died of diphtheria. If he and Lille were left alone together in the end, he'd know what trouble was. They were fond of each other, always had been, but she'd ride him like a two-cent pony. She couldn't help it. And now, this gift of freedom. He swallowed, nodded, and croaked, "Are you sure, Mother? Yes, I'll see Athena. It's some kind of a day, sure enough!" and he was down the steps at a leap, dancing into the yard.

Clara was glad she'd done it. The boy shone with the gratitude he couldn't speak, and she enjoyed Athena real well in moderation. Liberty wasn't her brightest child, but it was painful to see his name grow ironic as his freedom wore away. She'd have been surprised if she could have seen him pause in front of the house to push the swing he'd once hung in the tree for his sisters, and lean to touch the face of a big pink peony at the edge of the neglected flower bed. Best peony in town.

Lib remembered the day Mother had planted that peony, a day in June with Gracie, his lost sister, laughing in the swing and kicking her feet. He was sent to the pump to get water for the planting and he tripped and spilled it coming back, but the day was so pretty, a lot like this one, that Lille didn't even rag on him, didn't say it was just like him or wouldn't you know. They all laughed along with Gracie, who acted as though he'd done it for her joy alone, and he went back to the pump for more.

He set off at a run now, headed down the road to Odin's place next door. Odin and Athena lived in a one-story house with a screened porch, back from the road and lower, in what Perley speculated was some kind of glacier scrape. Odin would be off hanging around the store with the men, Athena piecing a quilt, likely, or turning shirt collars. She was so lonesome that she about talked your head off, so Mother would have given two people pleasure at one blow. Maybe he'd find something pretty, up Monument Stream, to bring home to her.

"Athena!" he called, knocking, "you home? It's Lib Nickerson. Mother wants to know if you could come up for a visit."

A small animated face appeared behind the screen door. "Lib, my land, is that you? And your mother wants a little visit? I'd enjoy to do it! Why, Odin's no company at all, don't know why I ever married him. How's she been this weather? I hear some about Lille from the scholars walking home past my house, they like a cookie after school, you know. They seem to think awful well of her. And so they should, she's a smart girl. You want to come in and set?"

This was the pause for which Lib had been waiting. "No, thank you, I'm on my way to check on that rowboat of mine, and I've left Mother alone, so she'll be hoping for you."

"Alone? Why didn't you say so? I'll get right up there. Awful nice day for a visit. Lemme just take my sewing, and a jar of preserves. Likely she hasn't had the strength to put much up the last few years. That diphtheria was a sad business, wears you out if it don't kill you. She like raspberry?"

Lib, fleeing, called over his shoulder that his mother liked everything, which in a wider sense was true. He pelted down the road towards the lake, raising a bloom of dust with every impact of his foot. And the lake in front of him, silver and dark and cold, was the way to his paradise, the green rowboat his magic carpet. He had its prow pulled up on the shore, now it was May and the ice out, but he hid the oars on the Currans' screen porch, at least till they came back for summer. Then nobody'd prowl around and mess with a person's stuff. His oars. The furnishings of the camp. He hadn't been in there often, they sat and chatted on the porch steps mostly, but they had interesting things. Set of moose horns, he'd take those if he was a burglar. Though on second thought they'd be kind of hard to hide, so he guessed if he was an actual crook he wouldn't. There was a hanging lamp made of colored glass, you could let it down and put oil in. He'd tried to describe it to Lille, who'd probably like it, but he couldn't do it well enough. Lots of books. A cot with pillows on it, embroidered all foreign, looking like they came from someplace far away and special. It was a fine camp, though not peaceful like the water.

"My word, if there isn't a skunk, Clara," Athena said. "You know you had a skunk under your bed?"

"I believe you've met," said her hostess. "You remember this lady, MacDuff. Come on out and say hello. And how's that raccoon of yours getting along, Athena?"

"What, Junior? First rate. Helps with the dishes sometimes, if you can believe it, though he's hard to organize. I called him Junior to tease Odin, y'know, but it was more of a tease than I anticipated. I thought I was saying that Odin looked like a raccoon, and he kinda does, don't you think, but now all those bums he plays with all day are asking him whether there's been some big daddy raccoon around the place in the last few months. Honestly!"

26

"Men," they said together, shaking their heads. "That gang's got some mischief up their sleeves," said Athena. "Odin comes in looking all important, and when a man is NOT important but has that look on him, something's afoot. Stranger than all, he says he don't know but he might come to church with me on Sunday. Odin in church! Do you suppose he's done something wicked bad or has he got some project so big he thinks he'll require God on it?"

"Oh Athena," said Clara, "you and Odin do put a relish in my life! Junior too. Well if I was to guess, I'd say it's the latter. I don't believe Odin's really wicked, do you?"

"Nowhere near wicked enough," said Athena, "he's just a big blowhard. Why else would a woman have to take up with raccoons?"

Lib rowed close to the shoreline, not because he objected to deep water but because he liked to get a good look at the plants and animals; he liked to stare down at the rocks on the bottom, their colors bright when they were wet; he liked to trade greetings with people onshore.

By the time he got to the Thoroughfare, folks he knew had sent his mother a bunch of flowers and a loaf of bread warm from the oven. Babies too young for school had waved.

"How's your pig shaping up, Lib?" a neighbor asked, man to man.

"Shaping up to be a devil," said Lib. "Can't wait to butcher him, and I think he's saying the same about me."

He was followed by the approving boom of male laughter.

And all the way, the water kissed and teased and slapped the flat bottom of his boat. "Lib," it said, "Lib," and loved him.

Up Monument at last it was all peace, the water calm and wide in the way of ancient streams and waterways. Lib shipped his oars and lay back, he breathed in his place on earth, his thin place. It smelled wet and cold, it smelled like soaked stems and last year's cattails, like evergreens alive and dead, like heron feathers and beaver tails (he

thought) and the sides of leaping fish. The skies were big all over
Aroostook, everyplace he'd seen, but when he gazed straight up at the
sky over Monument, it looked not only wide but deep, no end to it--
so deep, so endless, that any astonishing thing might slide down.

CHAPTER FIVE

"If we could just catch us that old lake monster," Ruby was saying, lounging downwind of his companions as they preferred, "we could make a pile a money and sit easy."

"How'd you figure that?" said a farmer who'd sat down to put off going home.

"Ruby's right for once, show the critter off to folks, charge admission. People come through here on their way to Houlton, people come play baseball, whatever, they'd want to have a look at that old Leviathan," said a whiskered veteran of the 20th Maine, getting into it.

"Big old thing he'd be, how'd you keep him?" said the farmer.

"Bigger question," said Odin, "is what'd we use for bait. Bait, and a hook."

Nutter, feeling sportive on his way to preach, smiled as he passed, and said, "The Lord himself will provide a ram, my son. Come hear about it."

"We could someway pickle him," said Ruby.

"Or dry him out," said the whiskered vet.

The church bell, not large but long saved for, began its dings.

"Well, whadaya think,' said Ruby. "Yes or no on the sermon? I don't aim to wash my hands at the pump and slick down my hair if you boys ain't coming too."

"Dunno," said Odin. "Yeah, I guess I better, though. I already told m'wife I might, and I'll get a better dinner if I do. She's a pain in my ass but she's some kinda cook."

"Thing is," said the one-handed vet, "that fool minister might get to be some use to us if we butter him up. You heard what he said when we was talking about bait, like God would provide, my son."

"That ain't really about bait," said the vet with the crutch, who'd had some Bible lessons, "it's about Abraham's going to kill his kid for a sacrifice and don't like to tell him so."

"What about Perley, we might get hold of him, he's a selectman, and ain't that about as good as a minister?"

"Hell, I'm a selectman," said Odin. "Perley's a good guy but he don't take us serious, he's just playing around. I don't think he even hardly believes in the great beast of the water, but if he don't, he's wrong. When I was on my voyage, I saw the beast myself, the very beast."

"What was it like?" said Ruby. Odin's narrative hook snagged him every time. The others shut their heads off.

"Longer than the great ship," said Odin, expanding. "Two times, three times as long, and sections of his back raised up in hoops that'd go right over the roof of the schoolhouse. Them hoops was all jagged like a castle wall and its edges was like blood. And when he raised his great head, his mouth opened as big as that stove in the store behind us, and all fulla flame so when he'd dive again, that water just boiled." It was a practiced recitation if somewhat uneven.

"You didn't say his eyes," Ruby prodded.

"His eyes," said Odin, "big as punkins, looked at us, ship and all, like he'd swallow us up, only he just eaten."

"What'd he eat, Odin?" Ruby cried, rapt.

"Oh, likely another ship. Now THAT was some monster, Boys, so I know for a fact that our own Leviathan can be swimming right here in East Grand Lake before our eyes, and I say he is. We got to get him. Even if we have to go to church."

"Now my brethren, if you are my brethren, and my sisters, if you are my sisters, let us speak of swords and ploughshares," intoned Joab, spreading his arms wide. His brethren and sisters (if they were) looked cautious, mindful of previous sermons. "Let us speak of war and peace," he went on, "let us speak of hatred and love. Let us speak of death and life. Isaiah 2:4 says that the people shall beat their swords into plowshares and their spears into pruning hooks, and they shall not learn war anymore. But Joel 3:10 says "Beat your plowshares into swords and your pruning hooks into spears: let the weak say 'I am strong.'" So which direction is it to be? And who shall tell you?"

Odin looked across at Ruby, raised his eyebrows, and mouthed "hooks," holding up his thumb and forefinger.

Ruby nodded slightly. His whole family was in church today, persuaded by Joab, and he was hoping his wife wouldn't take fits during one of the hymns. He liked to sing. Gladys, the front of her face washed, was hoping that if her mother did take a fit, her father wouldn't kick her and tell her to get up. She was sure THAT wasn't right, in church or out of it. As the family's most frequent church-goer, she had managed to steer them into a pew near a door, though her father generally preferred to be more prominent in any gathering.

Could you also beat a plowshare into a giant fish hook, is what I want to know, and where would you go to get it done? Odin was thinking, his mind all abuzz. He listened with as much concentration as he could muster, but it was just blather, no instructions. Had he ever seen it done on his voyage? Had they fished for sea serpents? It was a long time ago, but it seemed to him that they had. Had they hoisted the anchor and trolled with it? What would they have used for bait?

"Who shall tell you whether it's time for peace or time for war? Who shall tell you, I say?" The Reverend Nutter flipped his coat tails and laid his hand on his chest like a man about to take an oath. "Why, your wise leaders, your brave generals, and yes, your ministers, your holy men. We also are wise, we also lead you, Generals in our battle against Satan himself!"

Outrage hissed across the congregation in waves. Veterans of the great war of the Sixties turned red from the neck up. Children had heard grandfathers speak of their generals, of the wise and humorous General Chamberlain, of the great General Grant himself, in their tone a kind of worship otherwise reserved for God; they had been tucked into bed, as a treat, to the tune of General Butterfield's Taps. Now they looked with dismay at their parents, who were themselves sending black looks at the pulpit. Ministers were as good as Generals?

31

The shining Chamberlain, their family's hero, was no better than this nasty-looking man on the platform? Dizzy from a world turned upside down, two four-year olds in the front row burst into tears and vomited over their Sunday britches and stockings.

"Dropped the ball again," Lib mouthed at his sister. They were not joining the small company of queasy looking young people slipping out the door. Seasoned farmers and schoolteachers shrug at body contents. Anyway, the windows were open, and they wanted to see what Nutter would do with this turn of events.

"I was just saying—but alas," (here Nutter, smiling with visible effort, shifted his face into something intended as, but not quite achieving, pity) "I see that some of my smaller brethren are not feeling well." Lille noticed, amused, that he seemed not to be looking at them directly, that he was fixing his soulful gaze on a corner of the crown molding. "We are all enjoined to love little children and gather them up, but perhaps not the gathering up just now. No, we send them to their homes with love. We may speak again at a more propitious time of swords and ploughshares. Instead let us now join together in singing 'Onward Christian Soldiers.'"

"Nice recovery," Lille murmured. She and Lib were pleased, though not so much for Joab Nutter's escape. They liked to sing. Most of those remaining liked it. Ruby Wayne sent up a tuneful bellow. He hoped they'd sing "Faith is the Victory" next. Now there was a tune that got your ginger up.

The general-store gang crossed the street and went into a huddle.

"So a person can beat one kinda tool into another," mused the vet with the crutch, "though nobody better get hold of my sword, no sir."

"Nobody wants your sword," said Odin, "it would slide right through his lip. But how big should a hook like that be, would you say?"

"'Bout like them chandeliers in the illustrated papers," said Ruby, "and three or four hooks to it."

There was a general nodding. "Anybody got a good blacksmith connection some distance away?"

"Might have," said the vet with the whiskers. This was followed by the heavy breathing of conspiracy in progress.

"But look," said the vet who thought his sword had been disparaged and felt crabby about it, "are you sure a sea serpent kind of thing could live in a lake? It ain't the ocean."

Now Odin was insulted. "This ain't just some ordinary lake," he said, "it's damn near an ocean, or anyway a inland sea. Why East Grand Lake is twenty-five, thirty miles long, and nobody knows how deep!"

"Silas Peabody prob'ly knows," said Ruby. "My old man told me how his boat went down and he never come up. Must've got the anchor rope wound around his feet and gone to the bottom."

"Well that's useful," said the crabby vet. "Prob'ly the damn monster ate him. They like meat, Odin?"

"Oh yes," said Odin thoughtfully, "they eat meat." Maybe a ram wouldn't be a bad thing at that.

CHAPTER SIX

Geography lessons were bittersweet for Lille, who longed for Europe as a calf longs for milk. She was needed at home: let that get its teeth in your skirt-tails and you're done for. Her brother seemed content enough with a small world, provided it was watery. She imagined that Grace, the youngest, might have got somewhere finally, with Lille and Lib to back her up, but that was over, her turn had been too short. Lille didn't want to stay away forever, she just wanted to see things, ancient things, flashy things, things she hadn't thought of. And now here she went, trying to raise that hunger in the minds of these children who'd grow up to find themselves in the same fix as her, likely. But if they ever got the chance and didn't bother, that would be worse.

"Today," she said to her students, "let's talk about France. Did you find your geography books exciting? No? I'm not surprised."

She paused and relished the moment. The older two-thirds of the room had started their education under another teacher; Lille and Lib had endured her too, a woman vicious beyond metaphor, an insult to witches and rattlesnakes, and in all her own dealings Lille played counter to that teacher's venomous ghost.

"Geography," she went on, "shouldn't just tell us what a place is next to on a map, or what it exports or imports. That doesn't make anywhere seem real or interesting, does it." She didn't even mean it for a question. Book geography was dull, they all knew that, though sometimes, like Gladys, a child saw beyond it. But Lille planned to do

---

better than the books. "If you ever went there," she said, "how would it smell? What would you eat? What would you use for money? What does their language sound like?" She stopped; she could tell she had them.

"I have not been to France except on the printed page," she confessed, "but my first name, which you know is Lille, spelled L-i-l-l-e, is the name of a city in France, the northern part of France, and it's quite a big one. I'd like very much to see it. But who knows the name of the biggest and best city in France?"

Several of them did—"PARIS," they shouted. A big boy added, troubled, "Wait, ain't that a little no-count town downstate somewhere?"

"It is," said Lille, "though I'm not sure that in Leviathan we have much business to call other towns 'no count'—However," she qualified, dipping her head in deference to Harold, "we do have a very fine baseball field. And why would a small downstate town and the capital of France have the same name?"

Gladys remembered. "Towns name themselves after big places, don't they?"

Lille smiled at her, nodded, went on. "And when they do, they are sometimes pronounced differently. Calais, for instance, a hundred miles or so southeast of us, has all its letters pronounced when we say it, while in France, where it comes from, it's called Ca-LAY. Those final esses of theirs just break loose and slither off. So while we say Paris with all the letters pronounced, in France they say Pa-REE."

"What they want to talk so funny for?" said a twelve-year-old girl with all the sullenness of approaching womanhood. Lille scanned faces for signs of cognition.

Hugh, who had as usual been listening in, raised a polite hand. "But it wouldn't be funny there, would it, with everybody doing it. My grandpa said in the south the Rebs talked real drawly, they laughed at 'em when they weren't shooting 'em, he said, but after a while it began to sound natural." Comprehension flickered on the faces of his elders.

"Just right," said Lille, loving him. "Now French is a gentle, slippery sort of language compared to English; French speakers just seem to slide over their words." *C'est la vie,* she wrote on the board. "This is a kind of shrugging sentiment," she went on, pronouncing it, using her hands and shoulders in what she hoped was a French way, "Oh well, it's life, they say, shrug, shrug, so it goes. Now you try it. *C'est la vie.*"

She didn't know whether to laugh or cry at the sight of a roomful of Aroostook children, some surely headed for hard lives, shrugging off the hardness in a chorus of variable French. *C'est la vie, Gladys. C'est la vie, Harold. C'est la vie, Millie Goss, who won't blaspheme by saying it out loud.*

She moved on.

"Today," she said, "we're going to France in our imaginations, and fortunately it's a sunny day. No eye-rolling from the eighth-grade boys, please, your younger colleagues need you. Leave the schoolhouse gently, don't rock the ship." She could feel spirits lift, including hers. Lord, they must have been so bored, and patient with it. Even being out in the air when it wasn't recess helped. She pointed to the higher land across the road, to the gray and white headstones. "There you see the great city of Paris," she said. "We've crossed the Atlantic Ocean"—here she gestured to the lake—"escaping terrible sea monsters, and now our sailors—eighth grade to the oars, please— will take us across the choppy harbor to the mainland."

Seeing the little ones amused, being enlisted into the corps of adults, the big boys grinned and took the group's outside edges. The eyes of the little ones widened; they were still young enough to imagine for a moment that France was across the road. Two of the middle-sized boys feigned seasickness, leaning over the gunwales. "What do you think-- you're in church?" quipped Gladys, new growth for her too. Laughing, they scrambled up the slope and were restrained at the edge of the cemetery. *"La vie,"* Lille said, "is also sometimes good. Remember it."

"Observe," she continued, "the straightness of the Paris

streets. The French like things in rows, trees and shops. It makes their nice clean cities look even more spacious. We will walk very slowly down this street, Rue Cimetiere, Cemetery Street, at the end of which you will see le Tour Eiffel, the Eiffel Tower, only ten years old but already a world wonder, the tallest thing in France, over a thousand feet high. Higher than the tallest trees in the forests around your faraway home in Leviathan, Maine."

Caught up completely, they threw their heads back to admire the obelisk on top of the rounded hill where the winter dead were kept till spring. In truth it impressed them always, good and tall for Leviathan, incised with names of soldiers. But now they could hardly bend their necks enough. "What do you smell?" said Lille, moving them gently along.

"Flowers," said a child.

"Ah, the flower stalls in Paris are famous," Lille said. "All colors, in tall silver containers, out of doors. Close your eyes and see it."

"Not just flowers, perfume!" said an older girl.

"Yes," said Lille, "we are now passing one of Paris's many perfume shops. French perfume is the best."

"Wood and varnish," said a boy, needing the masculine.

"The wind is blowing from the Faubourg-St. Antoine quarter then, which specializes in cabinet making, and where the Marquis de Lafayette is buried in the Picpus Cemetery. Do you remember who he is?"

Some of them did. "Oh!" said one, "he really was French!" That was a bonus.

They arrived just on time at the gravestone of the Elias Baker family. Lille could have clapped her hands. "Now here we are," she said, pointing, "at the baker's!" Children who had that year learned to read, got it, their first literary joke, and howled. "French bakeries are famous for their bread and pastries. Boulangerie is the French for bakery. Let's sit on the grass and shut our eyes and see what else we can smell." She had spotted Perley, partner in this enterprise, approaching from the Haney Brook Road side of Paris.

"I can smell bread, I think," said Hugh.

"Something sweet?" said Millie Goss, who, inclined to disapprove of French frivolity, disapproved a little of herself just then for having senses.

"No, biscuits!" Harold cried.

And there was dear Perley, level with them now, carrying a pan covered with a towel, and to her astonished admiration wearing a beret. "Open your eyes, children," she cried, "for here is Monsieur le Boulanger, Mister Baker, who has a French treat for you!"

Perley whipped off the towel with a gesture so showman-like that she almost expected Oliver the Rabbit rather than the Leviathan version, devised between them, of pain au chocolat. She had bought chocolate to bake in the hearts of the biscuits, which seemed the quickest form of familiar bread. Some of the children were already hungry, some for good reason. "You and Susie had yours?" she whispered.

"Right when they came out of the oven," he whispered back, "and they're just as good as you said they'd be. We put some preserves in Oliver's and marked it, we thought it would be easier on his stomach than chocolate. Saved a couple for your mother and Lib. Yours is in this batch."

"Nibble carefully," Lille advised as she and Perley handed the biscuits around, "there's a secret treat in the middle." Beautiful their faces were, beautiful their eyes looking up. Beatific their joy when they arrived at the chocolate.

"And now do you understand," said Lille, "why people say that French food is the best in the world?" They nodded. No argument on that afternoon when la vie, for all of them, was outstanding.

"By the way, Perley," she said, "where in the world did you get that beret? Children, tourists, please note that all Frenchmen wear this kind of hat, called a beret."

"Susie and I took our honeymoon in Quebec City," he said.

Quebec City—there at least one might hope to go. She was so set on Europe that she sometimes forgot that. She must remember to tell the children, who were now cleaning their hands with their tongues, getting the last crumbs of biscuits au chocolat.

The twins walked on either side of her on the way back. "I will live in France when I'm a man," said Harold, thrusting out his small chest.

"Miss Nickerson," Hugh said kindly, "what was the biggest place you ever saw, so far?"

Her heart steadied. "I saw the sea," she told him, "I saw the ocean at Bar Harbor when I went home with a school friend. It was wild and blue and smelled like salt and looked like it went on forever. Thank you for asking." She had stared across the water, knowing that Europe was out there somewhere, only too far away to see with human eyes. But she knew plenty of people right here in Leviathan who had never even seen the ocean.

"What's that fool of a schoolteacher up to now?" said the vet with the crutch. "She appears to be giving them biscuits in the graveyard. Next thing you know they'll be digging somebody's bones up to see how it's going. What'cha call it—anatomy class. And how's that fool Perley mixed up with it?"

"Oh, I guess Manfred and Clara's girl won't go far wrong," said Ruby. "Our Gladys thinks a sight of her."

"Kinda too bad she's not the boy," said a lethargic farmer.

"Don't even think of it," said Odin. "If she was the boy she'd a kicked our asses and you know it." There was a pause in which he imagined it. "So," he went on, "swords no good, got no spears, what you reckon's the best thing for hooks?"

"I reckon cultivators," said Ruby, who was seeming smarter all the time, though not more industrious or any cleaner.

"Got an old one of Father's," said the vet with the crutch. "No use to me anymore, can't push it. 'Sally Vee,' as the Frogs say, 'that's life.'"

"Who the hell is Sally V?" said the farmer, "some kind of Canuck whore?"

"You might say so," said the vet, looking at his crutch.

CHAPTER SEVEN

Susie, Perley, and Oliver were sitting on the screen porch to catch the evening's scent of spring, the humans in rocking chairs and Oliver on the glider, which gave him a better view than his pillow on the floor.

"You should've seen those children when they smelled my biscuits," Perley said, bragging a little and knowing it.

"They were some good," said Susie easily, vernacular for the comfort of it. "You might make 'em again one day. Next time our girl's home maybe."

"Easy enough," said Perley. "Isn't that a wagon?"

"So it is!" said Susie, leaning forward. "I hope nobody's sick up to Clara's."

Nobody was sick. It was Odin's wagon and team, Odin driving and the whiskery Civil War vet on the seat beside him, Ruby with his legs hanging over the tail. Ruby kept looking over his shoulder, anxious, at some spiky thing on the wagon bed, maybe about the size of a potato barrel, horse blanket spread over it. Susie and Perley, excited as only those with quiet lives can be, once again thanked God for a screen porch on the Haney Brook side, and waved at their neighbors, who returned the obligatory salute. Tired, you could tell. They looked like they'd had a long day.

Even Oliver, sharing the excitement, thumped the glider with his hind foot. How did rabbits do that, Perley always wondered, whack a soft surface with a furry foot and make a crack like a palm on a drumhead. He bet you could hear it all the way to Odin's, all the way to Nickersons' maybe.

That was the idea. Oliver Twist wished he could tell Junior to watch out for something strange coming his way, something big on a wagon bed, but at least he'd thumped a kind of warning. Junior'd be alert.

"Got to get you out more, buddy," Perley said to the rabbit. "Full moon tomorrow, what you say we have a look at it?" Oliver nuzzled Perley's hand with deep affection, but he had his ears up, listening. Junior's excited chitter always carried.

And there it came, high across the field. Likely MacDuff the skunk could hear it too and, curious, would wander down the ravine when his folks were asleep. They had a cat door. Oliver wished he had a cat door.

"What the hell is that?" Athena said as the wagon rolled up to the barn. She had a porch too, she'd seen it coming. "What you got under that horse blanket, Odin? You been in Houlton all day or what?" She nodded goodnight to Ruby and the vet, who were scattering just in case, Athena's temper being well known.

"What, what, what?" Odin teased. "You keep a secret, blood swear?"

"Piffle, I guess I can if that layabout Ruby Wayne can. Can't even keep money in his pocket or his boots off his wife."

"Okay," said Odin, "never mind about Ruby, lookit here," and he raised the horse blanket with care and some reverence. He had discovered on the ride home from the blacksmith's that the thing was special in some way having to do with ambition. Until now he'd only cared for the past, for the big event of his long-ago Voyage. Now if they caught Leviathan, if that fancy hook worked, he'd be famous and maybe rich too. They'd hear his name all over the County. "Know what that is?" he said.

"Nope," Junior thought, clutching one of Athena's fingers like the child they'd never had, "but those are wicked big claws, keep'm outa MY hide!"

"Somethin' to cook with?" Athena guessed, thinking that there were only four pointed things, couldn't cook an awful lot on it, and have to hang it over the fire.

"No ma'am!" Odin was dancing something very like a jig. "Somethin' to CATCH with! We're gonna catch that Leviathan critter in the lake, make a whack a money. Nobody around here'll ever a seen anything like it."

"I guess not," said Athena, "considerin it ain't real!" Then she took a step back at the sight of Odin's face. "Okay, okay," she said, "what you gonna use for bait? A roast beef on every one a them hooks? You stay away from my coon!"

"I ain't gonna hurt Junior," Odin said, "he's my coon too, aintcha Junior. Could wind you around them hooks nice and pretty, though."

By that she knew that Odin was over the insult. Threats were their love talk. "Put the blanket back, why dontcha," she said. "Something could get hurt on them sharp points."

Joab was on his knees in his study. He said it was the study, his wife called it the breakfast room. One day he'd pointed out that she had never once served breakfast in there, and she'd countered with things that should not cross the lips of a Christian wife, ever, like who could eat breakfast in front of the engraving of that ugly John Knox, and when had he, Joab, ever opened his mind enough to put anything into it. What's more, the next day she'd put out a milk jug one of her infidel friends had given her, what they called a grotesque, mouth lolled open, tongue out. Who could pray with that thing looking on?

When he'd first kneeled he'd meant to pray, he wanted the answer to a question with which he was struggling. After fifteen minutes he'd realized he had his mind clenched against any answer except the one he preferred. That being the case, he had subsided to cold calculation and was now weighing the advantages of joining the boys on the steps in their scheme to catch Leviathan, if such a creature was there. Well, Psalm 104 said he existed and that was about all the sign he was going to get, he supposed, even if it didn't specify East Grand Lake. It was not so much the money, though if money

---

was to be made he could use it, given the possibility that he'd lose his church. The damnable children howled and upchucked whenever he opened his mouth. Suffer was the name for it. How could Jesus stand to lay his hands on those nasty little heads? That snip of a schoolteacher had sent him packing too, who did she think she was? And eating biscuits in the graveyard? Too smart for her own good.

He pulled himself back from outrage, if they caught that thing, if they caught it and put it on display, the children would value him then. If he could take credit as the leader of that exploit, even the Northern Baptist Convention would hear of it. The ends would justify the means. He would cast in his lot with the sinners and wastrels. If they'd let him.

"How much that thing cost us?" Athena wanted to know.

"Just the horse feed, and lunch for the three of us," Odin said, "That old vet with the crutch gave the cultivator for the hooks, and that old whisker-face one knew a blacksmith that was with him in the 20th but come away whole. Gave an old war buddy the labor for free. Ruby did all the heavy lifting, though it ain't like him to, and brought along the horse blanket."

"Whatcha gonna use for a line?" Athena wanted to know more things now; she'd gotten kind of interested. "You catch him, how you gonna haul him up? Can't get him in any boat I've ever seen. Gonna shoot him in the water?"

"I saw such boats in my youth," said Odin, on the edge of nostalgia.

"You better have some supper," Athena said. "Got time to think about it."

Odin threw his arm across her shoulder and they went in the house. Short man, short woman, large hook.

Oliver was the most intellectual of the animals, they all knew it though none of them had the words for it. The others—Junior, MacDuff, the cats—loved and admired him. But he had weaknesses: his paws were not much use except for digging, he couldn't work locks; and he was profoundly edible, in particular peril at night.

Junior was no brain trust but he had a lot to say and tones to say it in. If he was happy or indignant or excited you knew it, even the humans knew it. Also, his hands were terrific, he could do everything but drive a wagon, and he hadn't tried that. Although edible, he didn't look like an easy mark.

MacDuff was smart enough and sweet company, he'd always share and step aside, though you knew he didn't have to, he was a skunk. When you were with MacDuff nobody'd come near you if he even looked as if he might upend. Dogs let on they needed their sleep. Predators sidled off. The three of them were a power in the midnight neighborhood. Also, a barn cat or two sometimes came along and thinned out the field mice. Oliver found that somewhat disturbing, but a mouse is not a rabbit, he told himself, and one of those barn cats was just about as good with a door as Junior.

Tonight the whole gang came for him, cats and all. He'd learned to jump up and bump the hook out of the eye on the inside of the porch door, and Junior turned the latch on the outside. They ran in a pack, different gaits but they stayed together until they got to Junior's barn. Odin had left the tailgate of the wagon open and the canny raccoon had twitched off the blanket so his friends could see from floor level. MacDuff wasn't a good climber, though Oliver might have managed the jump. The cats hopped up and edged around it, wondering what it was.

MacDuff thought that it looked like a fishing thing but much bigger. He lived with Lib, after all, and had once been out in the boat and eaten an angleworm after Lib rinsed it off for him. He'd never seen a worm near that big, though, and didn't want to.

We look too small beside that thing, Oliver thought, and he turned his face to the path home. They all ducked their heads briefly to Junior, who had shown them pretty much the weirdest thing they'd ever seen. He'd be getting some paybacks from them in the next few days, he knew, though that wasn't why he'd brought them, or not altogether why.

44

Back at Oliver's house Junior turned the latch and let him in. Perley was sitting on the glider. "What the hell was it?" he said, "Some kind of big hook is what I'm guessing from the shape. Like this?" he sketched a hook on the air with his hand, not unlike Odin in church, thinking that Oliver might not know the word for it.

Oliver feared that he might be in for grief-- shut in, or worse, shut out. O Lord, what if he was dropped out in the cold world with no biscuits or gliders or love? He might as well dig a hole and die in it. What did Perley's strange hand gesture mean? He looked him in the face and saw that it was kind, even amused. "You thought I didn't know you were going out at night? I might have fixed the locks but I could see you were safe with Junior and MacDuff and that bunch of hoodlum cats. I haven't told Susie. We guys have to stick together, right?"

Right! Oliver, saved, stretched out across one of Perley's bare feet. It felt terrific to both of them.

In the back bedroom at Odin's Athena turned into his arms as they slept. "Leviathan," she murmured.

CHAPTER EIGHT

It was nearly full dark when the peddler got to Leviathan and started up Haney Brook Road, his packbasket lying heavy against his spine. He'd go sleep in someone's barn, and none of their damn business if he did. He knew which houses didn't keep dogs. He had as much right to get away from the damn black flies as anyone. Maybe he'd smoke in the barn too, leave the smell behind when someone came out to milk in the morning. That would give them something to get riled about. He expected people to think the worst of him.

About that he was right. Nobody likes a man so rotten with malice that he smells bad. Nobody trusts a man who hides his eyes. This one wore dark glasses like a blind man and the people on his routes were pretty sure he was faking. Didn't he shy rocks at animals with all the accuracy of a seeing man? He trampled flowers. He unbuttoned and peed in dooryards, bold as a crow. And his goods were shoddy, his patent medicines made a person feel sicker, his sewing thread broke, his chocolate was gray with age. He'd had a proper push cart once, but this time he had his stuff in a wheelbarrow with a canvas over it, and a pack basket, and nobody asked him why. Women and children on back roads sometimes checked him out in the name of novelty: he might have something they hadn't seen before. Or someone greeted him in passing because he was human, more or less; he existed.

In front of Odin's house the peddler paused. Junior, half way up a tree, remembered peddlers and chittered with irritation. The peddler bent to get a rock. He saw a nice sharp one, fairly good sized, just over the edge of the road into Odin's yard, but when he leaned to pick it up his load overbalanced him and he somersaulted down the slope into the scrub and wild vines, smashing his nose, gashing his skin. Before his neck snapped he had just time to think, *Goddam raccoon musta pushed me.* He lay on his back, having lost the packbasket in the process. Junior, who liked to jump on things, scrambled down, pleased, and jumped on the dead face until it was as good as unrecognizable. Under his feet the surface was irregular but pliant, it had a pleasant bounce. When he was through he washed the mess off his toes in a puddle and went inside.

Lib was having supper with the Currans, who'd come down for a couple of days to open camp, sweep the dead flies off the windowsills, brush down the walls, air it out. Seeing activity there, Lib had run home to get Eileen's gift, the beaver family he'd carved for her. He set it up on the table and she actually clapped her hands. She was a stolid, undemonstrative child, though clearly smart as blazes and warmhearted enough, so Lib felt well rewarded.

"This one's the mother!" she said, picking it up gently. "This one looks like the father. But who's that one?"

"It's the uncle," Lib said at random, "He's quite old so he lives there too. And that one's the neighbor lady who's brought over some tasty roots and weeds."

She laughed with a gurgle and stroked the neighbor lady.

"And that one's you," said Lib, "that small one holding a book." He was making it up, he hadn't thought of correlations and was surprised at his own invention. He wasn't around children all that much, not since Gracie and her playmates. Who, come to think of it (and he wished he hadn't), had been about the age Eileen was now. Eileen, who was looking at him with such adoration that he felt as though he'd won first prize at the State Fair.

"Stay and eat with us, Liberty," said Mrs. Curran, "and catch us up. We want all the winter gossip, please."

"Yes," said Lawyer Curran, "and tell us why two of the step-sitters were out front with a boatful of rope and a lantern last night, letting down an anchor and hauling it up. What were they fishing for?"

"Dreams," said Lib, and sat down. He felt, in this company, like a competent grownup.

Supper was cold ham and fried potatoes, with a dash of relish he'd never had before, and a lemon pie they'd brought with them from Houlton. Every family's cooking had a different flavor, he thought, which interested him.

"Now to get back to those men in the boat," Lawyer Curran said after the pie, "what sort of people are those boys who hang around together, would you say?"

"Oh," Lib said easily, "they're pretty good fellas," and then he stopped. He'd been asked a real question. "No they're not," he corrected himself with a grin. "Not very good, not very bad, but lazy and inclined to take the easy path. Odin's my neighbor, not bad but kind of full of himself. Ruby's not as foolish as he looks, but he's easy lured. I think some of the vets are still mad somehow, like they're owed something they haven't been paid. Now I say it, they're kind of a powder keg. One I wonder about, though, is the minister. Something off about him, he makes the babies cry."

"Bravo!" said the lawyer. "I always knew you were a smart man, Lib, and a wise one too. Why didn't your folks send you up to Ricker to school? I always wondered."

"Held back in second grade for too much looking out the window," Lib said, "so Father said I wasn't worth paying for and I didn't disagree. He couldn't get away fast enough after my little sister died, you know, kinda broke his heart, and he needed to leave a man behind, so that was me, I was fifteen then. He drops off a load of wood sometimes, and I've known him to help with the haying, but he still can't stand to be around us. Probably never will."

"Well, sir, you don't have to go to school to be educated," said his host conversationally, leaning back with his fingers laced behind his head. "You just help yourself to a book from here anytime, you know where we keep the key. Take it out in your boat if you'd rather. Give him that piece of oilcloth, will you Eileen? Ever read any Emily Dickinson? No? I think you two might get along."

Lib was stunned. He took the book and shook the man's hand, his eyes eloquent enough. He fled.

"You come around any day!" Mrs. Curran called after him.

"You're full of surprises," she said to her husband. "How'd you know enough to pick Dickinson, which by the way I think is just right for him?"

Eileen beat him to the answer. "Lib's got ideas he doesn't know how to say."

Her father picked her up and hugged her.

By the time Odin had listened to Junior and come out to see what had him excited, Lib was passing their house, almost home, wanting to think about his amazing supper with the Currans. Wanting to, but seeing Odin he paused as he'd been raised to do. He looked down into the ravine. "What the hell?" he said.

"I believe," said Odin thoughtfully, "it's some kind of a dead man. And a packbasket over there."

"There's a wheelbarrow up here," said Lib. "You see it happen?"

"Nope," said Odin. "Junior there come and got me. Smart coon."

"Huh," said Lib, "think it's anyone we know?"

"I believe," said Odin, "it might be that sonofabitch peddler that comes around."

"Probably went after Junior," said Lib. "He always gave our cats a pretty bad time. MacDuff not so much though. Pissed on mother's hollyhocks once, right under her window, and the skunk went for him. Blind's no excuse. If he was, which I doubt. Okay with me if he's dead."

"Okay with me too," said Odin thoughtfully, wicked ideas rising up like swamp gas. He and Ruby had just yesterday sounded the lake bottom to find the end of the ledge. That would be the place to lay the hook, they reckoned, not so deep they couldn't get it back, but right at the drop-off where the glorious and money-making Leviathan could swim over and snap up the bait. And now it looked like the Lord might have provided the ram after all, my son, just like that dipshit minister had said.

"See here, Lib," Odin said, "This peddler hasn't got anybody in the world as far as we know, not kin nor friend. Now I'm a selectman, and if you'll just do me a little favor I'll get two-three of the fellas together and we'll do a nice free burying up at the back of the cemetery. No trouble, he's not too fat and it's just across the road."

Lib did hope the favor wasn't taking one of Mick the Peddler's legs and helping to haul him through the scrub growth to Odin's barn. He imagined the way the body would catch on stumps and bushes, how it would jerk. "I'd appreciate it if you didn't mention this to home," Odin said. "It's a sensitive matter, kinda, what with no papers. Now maybe before you're in for the night you'd just go cross lots and send that minister over here. Ask him to hitch up and come with his wagon, maybe."

Lib, who'd never lived anywhere but Maine, rightly understood "maybe" to mean "Do it." He noticed that the minister looked sick but not surprised when he went to hitch up.

Joab Nutter thought he'd rather die than drive up to Ruby Wayne's shack in the dark, through the dark trees and God knew what else. But he did it, he was in too far to back out, his feet were set on the Paths of Wickedness. He was a town man too, and his horse was a town horse, and both of them sidled at the night sounds. When at last he saw the small illumination of Ruby's window, the one kerosene lamp with the dirty chimney, he was more than glad to tie the horse and knock. He'd have company going back to Odin's.

Ruby cracked the door open. Joab had never seen a more dismal room.

"Oh, Reverend," he said, "sorry to open the door myself. Gladys is to bed, and my wife's just had one of her fits, ain't you, Edna Mabel? Sorry you missed it. I just kicked her till she come to, didn't I, Sugar."

Edna Mabel turned her head on the table and shut her eyes.

"Odin send you? Said he would, if we got us some bait. Lord provided, I guess, eh what, Reverend. You call Gladys if you have another one of them things, you hear me, Sugar. I'm goin' out."

Together they headed off into the dark.

CHAPTER NINE

At Odin's house Ruby and Joab found the most useful of the veterans, the only one of the general-store idlers invited to the night's activities. Not only was the blacksmith connection his, so they owed him the hook, but he had a full set of working arms and legs. Affixing a dead peddler to a giant hook in the dark, Odin reckoned, would not be improved by the work of participants who tipped over at key moments or in their excitement reached out with phantom arms. Further, in his battlefield experience this vet had studied the mechanics of the newly dead, some of which he implied might be unexpected. It had been he who helped Odin wrap the peddler in a tarp.

"Now Reverend," said the vet, "I know Odin feels awkward about asking you, but we have here the body of a dead man—no, we didn't kill him!—dead by accident and identity unknown. It seems clear that he's come to us like the ram to Abraham, just when we need him. But Odin thinks, and I agree-- and I'm sure you do too, Ruby-- that it would be more dignified-like if he rode to the lakeshore in your rig, you being a minister and all. So Ruby will just get in the back of Odin's wagon to lighten yours."

Ruby lost no time in the exchange, while Odin and the vet

lifted the intended bait (heavier and more awkward by the moment, it seemed) and dropped it in the back of the minister's light rig. The sound of impact was unpleasant, leggier than a bag of grain, not as leggy as a deer. The horse, nervous, danced in its traces. Joab, burning with shame and rage, glancing over his shoulder for Satan, told himself that the thing under the tarp was Bait. Bait. Big, but only bait. These louts, these minions of the devil, had played on his ecclesiastical vanity to make him do a nasty chore. But there was no going back, he had set his hand to this grotesque plow. The irrevocability of hell, he supposed, might taste like this to the damned.

Odin's wagon held the three men, the four-prong hook with a dozen yards of stout chain attached, a coil of rope, and a number of tools that included a lantern, a chisel, and a hatchet. He'd hitched up his team; the horses kept each other calm. Not a good night for a whinny. He and Ruby had foreseen that the operation might be sensitive in nature, the bait not exactly legal. A neighbor's strayed sheep, say. Having been sent a human for bait exceeded his expectations: from here on in, the night was all adventure. There was half a moon, some cloud cover. The lake glimmered. It was about right.

"Catch aholt of that tarp," Odin ordered when they stopped, and Ruby leaped to do it. He aimed to be Odin's right-hand man and this looked like his chance-- Odin would be planning to work him pretty hard. He wasn't as lazy as people thought, he told himself, just hadn't found anything worth working up a sweat over till now. Joab, he saw, was of no account, only their cover in case anybody came by. Someone they could laugh at if they got antsy, him from away and thinking he was better than them. Odin and Ruby pulled the peddler off Joab's rig with a thump; the horse shied. Odin's stallion shook his mane in tough-guy contempt, and his mare snickered. "Shut up," Odin said, and slapped their haunches in a comradely way. As for Ruby, he was downright giddy, he'd never been anywhere or done anything much up till now.

"Let's get his clothes off him," said Odin. "Don't want to have to shove these hooks through cloth, do you." It wasn't a question.

Each of the four thought in secret that he didn't want to shove those hooks through anything, no he didn't. There was a pause. They rolled the peddler out of his tarp and peered at him in the dark. Would they draw straws for jobs, Ruby wondered.

"Shirt," volunteered the vet, who knew better than the others what things might pop up in the pants area: jack-in-the-box without the tune. He was leaving the pants for someone on whom a surprise wouldn't be wasted. He pulled the suspenders down over the stiff shoulders and dragged the shirt partway over the dead man's head, where it caught under his chin, a respite for the living. They were finding that face too pale in the dark, pale as bone, pale as the moon but it gave no light, it swallowed light. (Had they looked, it was not paler than Joab's. Damned lily-liver hadn't even climbed down to join them, Odin thought.) Now the vet yanked. The cloth ripped. Loons shrieked with derision.

Odin, who caught on fast, called boots. He went to work on the peddler's feet, jerking the body as he freed them, ugly with bunions. He was glad to be in the fresh air on this job, but even so he turned his face aside. His stomach flopped. "You could have washed your feet, Mick," he said. He kneeled down and rinsed his hands in the lake and rubbed them over his face. An excuse to get farther from the peddler, to turn his back.

The bait had been more manageable without a name.

"Okay," Odin said, low, "we better hurry this up. Anyone sees us, we're goners. Looks like the pants are yours, Ruby."

The vet, anticipating, smiled into his whiskers. "You just unbutton him," he said.

"I got no truck with nobody's pant buttons!" Ruby protested, too loud.

"Shut up, you got to do it, it's your turn, ain't it his turn, Reverend," Odin said.

"I'm afraid it is, Ruby," said Joab, knowing whose turn it would be next if Ruby refused. "Shall I say a little prayer and ask our Lord to give you courage?" He guessed "our" was more or less all right, Ruby wasn't much good but he came to church.

"Maybe you can just rip 'em open, Rube," the vet said softly. He couldn't wait. He was pretty sure what would jump up and say howdy, and he stood behind Ruby to clap a hand over his mouth if he yelled. Sure enough, the bait hadn't been dead long enough to go limp again, and Ruby jumped so much higher than expected that the vet missed his mouth and cracked him in the Adam's apple.

"It's lookin' at me!" Ruby croaked, "Make it quit!"

"It'll quit," the vet said. "Didn't you know dead guys stiffen up there too? You shoulda seen'em after Gettysburgh and them places. Regular old tent poles. Sometimes the girls would come out with their handkerchiefs to see if there was any good left in them, wanted babies don't y'know." He thought he remembered that, he had a clear picture. Might have been a story. And how come his language had dropped back to farm boy? He hadn't said "them places" for close to forty years.

They swung around at a thump behind them. Joab had fainted and fallen backwards into his rig. His horse snorted. Odin's team gave him a sympathetic look. *Humans!*

"O Lordamighty," said Odin, disgusted, though he'd been more startled about those girls' handkerchiefs than he planned ever to admit. "Throw some lake water on him, Ruby, and some on your own head too, and then fetch the hook outa my wagon. I'll haul the peddler's pants off by the ankles."

That too was a bumpy process. Pants had gotten narrower. Why couldn't the sonofabitch have worn overalls?

Naked, Mick who was once a bad-tempered peddler lay on the cold grass, repugnant, shameful, but no longer Other. Of the men present only the vet had once read Lear's line about the poor, bare, forked animal that was man, and he had forgotten it. But they all sensed it—"thou art the thing itself"—Mick's ugly body was what all men came to. The tone changed a little, but not the plan. Now they were hiding a man's body in the lake, not just enticing Leviathan. All the same it would be improvident not to hide him on the hook, even Joab could see that. They set about it. The chisel and axe were no longer possible, a man wasn't cut bait. They'd have to fit him on.

What would bend and what wouldn't? Odin calculated that they could match him with three of the hooks, maybe. He thought he'd thrown a measure into the wagon bed. Neck? Gut?

Half an hour later, and a moon rising, they knew that stripping an engorged peddler was going to have been the easiest part of that night.

Odin and the vet had each taken an arm, Ruby had held the feet out of the grass. It was important that nothing look like the path of a dragged body. Foot-trampled grass might be anybody's work, someone setting night lines maybe. "Hold 'em up, Ruby, hold em up," Odin coached from sheer love of bossing, and Ruby tried. But he didn't much like where he had to look, even though the thing had gotten floppy, just like the old soldier had said it would. It still reminded him how he'd felt when they'd laughed.

"Let's set him down for a minute," Odin said. "We're near the edge of the water. Get down here, Reverend, and bring the hook out of my wagon. Yes you can too carry it, it's nothing but cultivator blades. Well, there's the chain, but you can drag that. Look just like a damn ghost, wontcha." He laughed at his own joke a little wheezily. Joab didn't. "So the thing," Odin went on, "is do we want to do this in the lake, and not have to drag him any farther once he's on, well maybe a little farther, or will it be harder to hook him on in the water?"

"Yeah, put him in," said the vet. "Number one, we don't have to hold his weight up then. Number two, likely some stuff will come out of him when we ram the hook through, and we won't have to clean it up, it'll wash out if the offshore breeze holds up. Here, don't let the bait float off!"

Joab followed them, dragging his chain, thinking damned was the right word. He was in the power of louts and fools, and even from them he got no respect. Bad enough the children hated him, bad enough his wife didn't honor him, but these! He stood on the pebbled strip between grass and water. "I still have my shoes on," he fussed. He meant, "I intend to keep them dry."

"Well take 'em off, Fool," the vet said, not disagreeably. Another blow, Joab thought-- to be called "fool" when it wasn't even abuse! He set the hook down and untied his laces with a gentleman's deliberation. Then he stripped off his socks while the others waited. He was almost pleased when the small rocks hurt his feet: penance. Were the others thinking of penance? He didn't believe so. "Roll up your pantlegs," said Odin. "You're coming in."

They laid Mick down at the shallow end so he wouldn't float off after they'd gone to all that trouble. He moved a little with the water. When he was good and firm on the hook they'd drag it in deeper. Very deep, in fact, given what they were fishing for!

"I'll tie the rope to the end of the chain and then hitch it to a tree back in that little grove," Odin said, "because I know how to tie sailors' knots, see. When I was on my voyage—"

"Hush!" said Joab sternly. "I think I heard someone on the road." There was nobody, nor did Joab in truth believe there was, but he had with one move curtailed Odin's brag and restored something of his own authority. If he persisted in sin (and so far he saw no way to quit), he might become a better strategist. At least with adults.

They looked at Mick. And the hook. "I think," said the vet, "that the space between his neck and his gut might be about the same as the space between two of those hooks." Ruby and Joab backed up some. Maybe they could sneak back to Joab's rig.

"Yes," said Odin. "You two get back here. Lay him out beside the hooks to see if he'll fit. Yeah. I believe the belly first, for the balance. I conclude it may take all four of us to push him on. No, all three of you. I'll hold the hooks steady, you all push him. Shove down hard and don't quit until the hook comes through. Probably want to duck the back bone and ribs and all."

Harder than they could have imagined. Worse. Mick was cold and wet and gelatinous and resilient, all at once. They pushed, trying not to leave their hands over the spot where the hook would come through. Trying not to let it get caught in Mick's dark caverns. They sweat in the cool air. "There!" cried Joab with a start, and the dead man's skin rose into a peak.

"All together," Odin cheered, and it burst through skin, bringing with it the unsavory stops on its journey. Dark fluids, oily on the water. The vet in after years, such few as he had, could never work out exactly what they'd hit.

"Now the neck," Odin said.

"Now you," said the others, "and we'll hold the hook steady."

The neck felt like a roll of gristle and Odin gagged but persevered. Two hooks loaded. They looked at the dead man's right leg, the one nearer the third hook. Joab spoke up and sealed his brotherhood. "I believe," he said, "that we could just hook his knee over the crook, and let the other leg dangle."

"Spinner!" cried Ruby, and there was laughter.

They pulled the baited hook as far as they could into the water and then, as the ledge grew steeper, they stepped back and let its weight pull it downward.

"Okay," said Odin as they left the water, "we'll better stroll along here whenever we can and cast a look at the rope. We don't know whether Leviathan will thrash like an eel or hang like a hornpout, so we'll take turns to come at night and feel it for heavy. Not you, Ruby, you're too far off and I got a special job for you. I'll put the wet clothes into a feed sack I got in the wagon and you throw it far into the woods up to your place, or bury it if you'd rather."

Too tired to talk further, they dripped back to their horses. Ruby looked at Odin, looked at Joab. He hoped he didn't have to walk home in the dark toting that wet sack, though he did feel that he'd had a sure-enough adventure, and that pleased him. Odin tasted responsibility. He felt like more of a boss than he'd ever been. Ruby was his worker.

"I might as well give you a ride, Ruby," he said. "Seeings how I'm all hitched up."

Ruby grinned. Odin, a sure-enough Selectman, was offering him a ride!

The vet was thinking, "Danger and dead men, by jiminy! I'm alive again."

Joab considered outer darkness.

And Mick the peddler, all his walking over, was washed, feet and all, in the darkness of the lake, where for the first time something might be going to find him desirable.

CHAPTER TEN

"They want you to what?" Susie hooted.

"Ain't a selectman about as good as a minister?" Perley quoted, amused. Odin had shared that remark with them, back on the day of the Plowshares sermon. "Seems they haven't seen the Reverend Nutter since yesterday morning, when he preached that short sermon, not much more than some crazy announcement about Leviathan rising out of the lake in the Rapture, can't seem to get his mind off the damn Rapture. Crazier every week. Nobody missed him till they remembered they'd want him for the Decoration Day Prayer in the graveyard. Course he may show up yet-- I'm hoping. Never thought I'd say that."

"I know," Susie said. "You'd most rather dig a grave than pray over one, wouldn't you?"

Dig? Oliver thumped once to stay in the conversation. *And ain't a rabbit at least as good as a spade?* he thought, *and they've never once asked me to help dig.*

"You can help me turn up the garden," Perley said to him, and reached under the table to stroke his ears.

On the cemetery rise, watched with envy by Lille's scholars, who were eating their lunches in the schoolyard, the women of the town were decorating graves with baskets of lilac and whatever else was growing in yards or woods. Though Decoration Day was meant for decorating the graves of soldiers, it was a rare woman who didn't slip a few flowers onto her own civilian dead while she was at it.

Not only to the children but to Lib and Lille's generation, the end of the Civil War, 34 years ago, seemed to have happened in another world; people wore different fashions there and had different ideas. Clara Nickerson, in her forties, had a clear memory of Appomattox but was not much touched by loss. Her uncles had made it home, then picked up and moved west. Petersburg was 35 years back, along with the terrible battle of the Wilderness that could still make tough old men weep down their beards, remembering comrades and brothers who burned there, screaming. Gettysburg, at which the 20th Maine had distinguished itself, was 36 years in the past. It was a thing in books, to women who hadn't known the dead. It was already history.

Carrying baskets for Decoration Day, some women remembered other baskets, handmade paper baskets with penny candy or flowers inside, hung on their doorknobs on May 1st by these dead boys who could run like the wind then, and you let them catch you so they could kiss you. Some of the girls on whose doors boys had hung Maybaskets were also among the dead, and others would die ere long. The girlfriend of Isaiah Ledbetter, the boy who'd been sold as a substitute by his father and likely died in the flames of the Wilderness, had herself died since the last Decoration Day, still mad enough to spit bullets. It was an unspoken relief to decorate without her fury around their ears, though the women had been sorry for her up to a point and could probably remember her with more sympathy soon.

"Isn't that a new grave over there?" somebody asked, pointing. "Hasn't got any kind of a marker."

"Oh," said Athena, "some fool of a man probably buried his old dog or his prize sheep."

Nobody argued. On Decoration Day women bonded in their ambivalence. They grieved the loss of their brothers and husbands and sons, touched of course with pity and pride, but also with some small secret irritation at their marching off and giving up their lives, which would no doubt have been useful at home. When one of the younger women announced that she'd like to know just what the men were contributing to the event anyway, Susie looked up, all innocence, and said, "Men? Men? Why, who do you think did the killing?" All her neighbors remembered why they loved her.

On the steps of the store the layabouts, the plotters, the men, in short, had thinned out. The vets were home polishing their swords and buttons, checking whether this year they could still climb into any of their gear. They'd be getting to the cemetery if they could, and hearing the tributes to the Union dead. Odin and Ruby and some stray farmers were looking grim. Odin was the only one of them who'd been in the war and he'd joined the Navy, hoping to recreate the central excitement of his boyhood. His warship, whose name he wouldn't speak, had been confined in its battles to the rivers, not uncommon but it filled him with shame and bitterness. For him the whole war had been a travesty.

"We're going to catch that bejeezely Leviathan if it's the last thing we do," he growled to Ruby, "and we're going to bleed him out and dry him up and nail him around the walls of the town meeting room, run the nails right through him and charge admission."

Ruby moved a little farther away. He was going to the ceremonies when they began, he'd been just too young to join up. Why was Odin so snarly? "You think we might better skin him out?" he said. "Don'tcha you think he might get to rotting? Mighty big body."

"Look here," said Odin, "who's ever laid eyes on a sea serpent, you or me?"

"You have," said Ruby, "or so you say." That was desperate. He admired Odin and in fact believed him, always had, but a man couldn't let another man disrespect him in front of a bunch of farmers, he knew the rules. He walked off to pump water on his head and slick up.

"Oh mercy," Susie said. She'd gone to stand beside Perley. "They're going to read from those dead boys' letters home like they always do. It makes me cry."

"Me too," said Perley. "Dammit."

The women assigned to read placed themselves behind the markers of the boys whose letters they held, or rather copies of copies, the originals having begun to wear out a quarter century back. Their job was to call up departed voices.

"Here is how we stand guard," the first reader began. "The Corporal stands guard 20 hours of the 24 and the Sargent stands 4. I like to go around among them and have them halt me, and give them the counter sign over the point of a bayonet. They do the guard business up brown. I never was so rugged as I am now. Had the mumps and stood guard the whole time. It was so warm yesterday I saw a man faint away but I stand it first rate.-- John J. Herrick, killed at Mine Run, November 29, 1863, buried on the field, Age 20 years, 3 months, 12 days."

"Dear Sister," read the second, "It was not till now that I heard Father was dead. Let me know how you get along at home. I should like to be up there now to help put in the crops, I could do two mens work. I am sending you my face in a frame so you don't forget how handsome I am. Tell Dana to be a good boy and I will fetch him a present when we come home. Give my love to all the friends.-- Isaac Freese, killed at Rappahannock Nov. 7, 1863, Age 26 yrs."

"I heard last night that Sally was married," said the reader from behind a stone with a marble hand, its finger pointing up. "O Lord that I ever enlisted and left those desirous girls that wanted a good man. I have not seen a girl in two months. Give my love to Plumey Estabrook and tell her to write to me, and give my love to Ida and Abbey and tell them to write. And Mary Jane is married too, don't that beat the devil. I fear before I can get back they will all be married to the home guard. I am sorry to hear Mr. L. hurt himself but tell him to keep off the girls and he will not get hurt, and when I come home I will try to take care of them if there's any left.-- Daniel Madigan, decapitated at Gettysburg, July 3, 1863, buried in Pennsylvania, Age 19 years, 7 months, 14 days."

"I am owed six months pay now and when I get some I shall send yours by express. I would like you to send me some clothes for winter, about three shirts and two pair of drawers and three pair of stockings when we get in camp for the winter. I want homespun shirts on account of rheumatics, they will keep me warm. Get some nice ones for me if you have to buy them; get some like those that the Fosterville women made, they will not fade as the checkered ones do. The drawers I want in particular whether they are knit or wove, just as you think best." Otis Hennessy, died of a congestive chill in Baltimore, October 16, 1864. Age 30 years.

"It about kills me the way they all had plans," Susie whispered through a hiccup.

"I know," Perley said, squeezing her hand. "And we haven't even got to Isaiah Ledbetter yet. Why do they put themselves through this."

"Oh lord," said Susie, "that poor Isaiah Ledbetter!"

The vets looked harrowed too. Together, various parts damaged, they had the look of hard-used toys; those among them with a knack for simile saw that and resented it. Moreover, the next man, though he'd come home to die of chest injuries, had been a jolly companion while he'd lasted.

"I have been here at the Baltimore hospital 15 days and have laid in bed most of the time but am getting more strength now. Too soft a place will make you sick and that is all that's wrong with me, having this good bed. If I had gone outdoors and laid a night or two I might have picked right up. You said Ned Wiggin got a letter saying I was wounded but pay it no mind. I was just wore out from marching. I want to hear from the draft, when you write tell me the names of all of the Amity boys that had to come. It would do me a power of good to hear of some of them lads coming out here to smell some of that southern powder. Tell Nettie to write.-- Joshua Merrill, died at home from wounds, Sept. 8, 1868, Age 27 years, 3 months.

Now they were for it. Perley squeezed Susie's hand. The story that had always grieved Lille chewed at everyone, a sore place that had to be touched. Isaiah Ledbetter, sold by his coldhearted father (a man related to more Leviathan folks than cared to own it), went to war in place of a doctor from Caribou who'd been drafted. The father pocketed the three hundred dollar substitution fee and then got a pension when the boy was killed. There was not one redeeming feature in the whole story except for the small gift of some spruce gum, a taste of home.

"Uncle, I take pen in hand to say I was glad to get the gum Aunt Marthann sent me. I do not think Father will send me any gum for he don't seem to care much about me. You said you wished you was here I am glad you are not for I do not want you to suffer like the men do here. If they draft in Leviathan I want you to write and tell me who is drafted, we had a fight and this regiment suffered more than any other regiment in the field. We lost 92 killed and wounded. I have no more to write so goodbye for this time.-- Isaiah Ledbetter, missing in action, The Wilderness, May 1864, real age 17 years."

There followed some clearing of throats and blowing of noses. Isaiah's history still stirred up grief and rage.

No sight of Joab Nutter yet. Perley began to compose a prayer in his mind, looked like his number was up and him still near to crying. Curse the man anyway. *Lord of battle,* he tried, *and Lord of peace. (Say something about the dead boys now.) In whose keeping our sons and brothers lie? We thank you that they died for victory. Help us to pity the enemy who died for failure? (No, they'd kick his ass for that, some of them seriously would.) Lord of battle and Lord of peace, in whose keeping our sons and brothers lie. We thank you for the lives that sustained the Union. We keep faith with them until we see them again at the greater celebration in the life everlasting. (Not too shabby, if only it wasn't all smoke and persiflage.)*

But there came the mad minister himself, scrabbling up the slope in his sermon coat with his hair flying. The drawing back was more embarrassingly general than any one of them had foreseen. Only Perley stood his ground. He'd nearly been put in as a sub himself just now.

"Perhaps," said Perley, "Mr. Nutter would like to give the concluding Decoration Day prayer." He stood back with Susie then.

Joab stretched his arms toward heaven. A breeze rose to shiver his coat tails.

"Raise up thy servants, O Lord!" he cried. "The dead in Christ shall rise first! And after that the most faithful among the living! Come, Lord Jesus, come soon! Amen!"

Small children, remembering him, moved closer to a parent.

"Con-sarn it, Reverend," said a one-armed vet, "let them poor boys down there get some rest. They died mighty tired and they ain't been dead near long enough yet."

CHAPTER ELEVEN

After Decoration Day came the first baseball game of the season, circumstances permitting, which is to say no snow on the field, no downpour, no Biblical plague of frogs or locusts, no chicken pox. Decoration Day was about death, though perhaps every year a little less about mourning, a little more about spring coming whether one was mourning or not. Baseball was the hope of summer, was the prodigality of knocking the ball out of sight, flinging the bat, running and sliding in the dust. Women cared less about it than men did, but they cared—they sat idle in the fresh air, their cakes were raffled and praised. Sometimes Perley cranked ice cream and Lib spelled him. Children and dogs, yapping with joy, chased errant balls into the tall grass.

Lille remembered that last year a certain Amity player, the fit of whose baseball pants she had noticed with approval, had winked at her, not guessing that it was the pants themselves she coveted, not their contents. Never mind, if she and the player met they'd laugh, a new world was coming. In any case, if she skipped the game she'd have to listen to its every play described on Monday, over and over, especially by Harold Smith. That settled, she constructed for the raffle her usual baseball cake, Necco wafers laid out for bases on chocolate frosting.

"Sure you don't want to come along, Mother?" she said. "I'd estimate you're strong enough now if Lib and I help."

"I'm afraid my resurrection would be too distracting," said Clara, "I'll skip the big game until you or Lib decide to play."

"Too bad for you, then," Lille said. "I'm not playing baseball until I can play it in pants like the boys. And Lib likely won't play until he can row bases instead of run them."

"Alas," murmured Clara, tongue in cheek, scooping MacDuff into her arms. "You don't want to see any old baseball game either, do you, O Chief of Skunks?" He did not.

Emmeline Nutter looked out the rectory window and across the unmown meadow to the baseball field. Sports didn't interest her. Ice cream did, a little, for the novelty of it. Likewise humans unconstrained by pews.

"You've no business to attend a frivolous game with heathens and infidels if you decline to visit the sick with me," said the sour voice of the Reverend Nutter. He very much disliked the sick himself, as his wife knew, though he had no idea that she knew. She knew also that he would have liked to make her share the unpleasantness, to baptize her into it by total immersion; she could imagine all too well the tone in which he was telling himself that such an experience would be to her spiritual benefit. Sickrooms didn't bother her one way or the other, in fact, but he could keep his sweaty hands off her soul. There was such a thing as spiritual lechery.

"Heathens and infidels my foot," she said. "Three quarters of those people put up with your sermons every Sunday." She'd go to that ballgame.

Wordless with indignation, Joab hawked into his handkerchief and dropped it on the kitchen table. He put on his ministerial coat and stalked out.

Having cast his handkerchief into the woodstove with the fireplace tongs, she put on the smart red jacket he'd forbidden her to wear in Leviathan (the devil's color) and strolled down the road to the gathering. She had made no friends in town, but she spotted an empty seat on the bleachers beside Lille. Chatting up a rural schoolteacher, what had she come to, Emmeline asked herself. But the teacher wasn't wearing proper corsets, by the look of it, which was bold. Bold but also very unfashionable, for which she had an eye. Joab would hate, but be unable to describe, the double impropriety. She looked at the seat, then at Lille, who cocked her head towards it. Emmeline sat down.

She smiled a little. "So you're the girl who sent my husband packing. I thought he'd eat that note he was so mad."

"Deserved it," Lille said shortly. "Stirred the little ones up just to make a show. Took me half the noon hour to tell them why Jesus wasn't going to carry off their mothers. If that husband of yours had got hold of them for his Bible lesson, they'd be crying yet. That was one hateful sermon, and don't tell me you didn't think so too. I saw your face."

Emmeline raised and lowered her eyebrows and smiled a secretive smile. She couldn't exactly be friends with a soft-shelled schoolteacher, but she was liking Lille's flavor and she liked having been noticed. "You ever been to Portland?" she said. "That's where I'm from."

"Nope," said Lille. "Went to school in Waterville, though. Coburn."

"Good school," said Emmeline, "I know the territory," and then, topping her, "I went to Oak Grove Academy."

"Good school too," said Lille, right back at her, "Vassalboro, I believe." Waterville was better, a college town.

Honors even, they gazed at the players, Amity's and Leviathan's. The latter team was just then being photographed at the edge of the field, the young men leaning on their bats, or rather three of the eight were leaning on bats. There looked also to be four gloves, one mask, one mustache, and a manager or coach, slightly older, not in uniform. Amity, the larger town, would be a little more fully equipped—more gloves, say; possibly more mustaches.

"Who's that," said Emmeline, "the dark, good-looking one who appears to be playing bare-handed?"

"Wallace," said Lille. "He says the glove gets in his way, and anyhow his hands are so calloused after the spring river drive he hardly needs it. Cousin on my father's side, incidentally. Good family, I'll introduce you if the Reverend has a one-man Rapture. But if you think he's handsome, how about the catcher for Amity?"

Emmeline drew in her breath. "So here we are," she said, "the schoolteacher and the minister's wife, being bad. This feels like being with friends in Portland, a little. You?'

"Like being young in Waterville, some," said Lille. "But I don't imagine we can ever do it again."

"No," said Emmeline, "I suppose we can't," and she chalked up one more mark against Joab.

The weather stayed fine, sunny with a breeze off the lake. Perley, though he passed it off as a gesture to the minister's wife, sent Emmeline a dish of ice cream because he felt sorry for her and admired the bravado of her jacket; he sent one to Lille from Oliver the rabbit, who was fond of her. Ruby Wayne bought one for his daughter, to her great surprise; dust clung to her even more when she was sticky, but neither of them cared. The Smith twins had saved up their pennies for the opening game and for the first time bought their own ice cream, feeling grown up and capable.

Frank Putnam retrieved enough balls from the weedy lot behind the outfield to keep the game supplied; some could remember early days when they'd had to pause and hunt. Lille's cousin Wallace made three jubilant home runs, and the men on the steps argued about his chances at Major League tryouts.

"Blessed if I don't think he could make it," Odin said. "And I seen some athletes on my voyage."

"Mermen?" said a sarcastic farmer, but Odin just smiled.

"Hit homeruns with their tails," he said, and got the better laugh.

"Who's the serious Amity child that seems to be acting as scorekeeper?" Emmeline said, licking her spoon for the last taste.

"Ah, that's my cousin William," said Lille with a note of pride. "He's Wallace's brother, been a whiz with numbers since he was knee-high. They're Amity people, but Wallace, who likes the underdog, is batching it up the road with some other boys who work in the woods, so he can play for Leviathan. Must say I'm grateful not to have William in school myself, he's way ahead of me in math, though I think he'd be polite about it. He and that first-grader of mine, Hugh Smith, are going to amount to something."

At the Seventh-Inning Stretch, just when Lille was tiring of baseball and the men on the steps were fixing to sing "Take Me Out to the Ballgame," a most remarkable thing rattled down the Houlton road, astonishing in its way as Ezekiel's fiery chariot. It was lawyer Curran and an enterprising Forest City blacksmith in a carriage with no horses: people looked at each other drop-jawed, full faced, but only slant-wise at Emmeline, for they remembered Joab Nutter"s diatribe against the 20th century and its shocking vehicles that would "eschew our friends the horses." Here, apparently, was one of them! It pulled up behind the bleachers and coughed to a stop. Curran stood up and bowed. "Timed it right, I hope?" he said. "This is Mr. Amos Farrell, the driver and maker, who deals in miracles." Amos Farrell, modest, looked at his feet and smoothed his mustache. He loved the praise, he'd always said this was possible to do.

People climbed the bleachers, they stood on the steps of the store, they flocked as near as they dared and reached out tentative fingers. It was indeed a carriage, the tufted black leather seat, the spoked wheels, the step up on the side, the protective panel in front, but where were the horses, where were the reins? The children, and some men, squatted and looked under the floor, as if horses might be hiding there. They stood up and gazed at a rod rising from the carriage floor, with a kind of handle on the top. How could that move the thing, they wondered, was it some sort of pump? Lille and Lib found themselves shoulder to shoulder beside the lawyer, Emmeline close behind them.

"Modern!" thought Lille.

"Fast!" thought Emmeline.

"It would not kick me," thought Lib.

"Your friend has brought the 20th century," said Lille to Lib in a tone of manifest gratitude.

"It makes a change," Curran said to Lib, and winked.

Lib Nickerson knew Lawyer Curran? The advent of this strange carriage seemed in some way to swing around Lib, not generally a pivot in Leviathan. He found his young cousin William at his elbow. "No hooves, Cousin Lib," said the boy, pleased for him. How had he known?

"I'll get out of the way so you can start your inning," said Curran. "How about we run it up Haney Brook Road and turn around in your dooryard, Lib? Want to come along? Or how about you, Miss Nickerson? Are you staying to the end, or can we give you a ride home? You can take my place and I'll stay and catch the finish."

"I'd trade the whole of the game for a ride in this—what are you calling it?" Lille said. "Hope Mother's looking out the window when we get there."

"I'm calling it Carrus, for chariot, if you know your Latin," Curran said, "maybe Car for short when I'm better acquainted with it." Lille smiled. She knew her Latin. "Be sure to toot your horn, Amos," he went on, "that'll call Mrs. Nickerson out."

It wasn't that the thing went faster than horses could, not good trotting horses such as Leviathan was fairly short of, but it felt more free, and the sweet wind in their faces was a marvel. Lille thought she had rarely been so happy, and Lib beamed on the other side of Amos Farrell. Only afoot or in the boat, he realized, had he ever moved without the rump of a horse before his eyes. He was singing in his head the rude stanza, loved by little boys, of "The Old Gray Mare, She Ain't What She Used to Be"—"The old gray mare she shit on the whiffletree!" He reveled in the absence of fresh horse poop.

Almost too soon Farrell's horn brought Clara to the door, though MacDuff at its unfamiliar sound had withdrawn to the bedroom, and the hired girl was clouding the kitchen window with heavy breathing.

"Strangers and Wayfarers, where do you hail from?" Clara called, laughing with them.

"From the future!" said Lille, standing tall before she jumped down. "And this clever man, Mr. Amos Farrell, has invented the 20th century and given us a ride in it!"

"Will you come in, Mr. Farrell?" Clara offered, but he stroked his moustache and bowed his head while Lib explained that they were expected back at the field. "Maybe you'd pump him a drink, then, Lib," she suggested, and that was done, for the roads were dusty.

The hired girl carried MacDuff back to Clara and put him in her arms, a brave first for both girl and skunk, but they could see that the occasion demanded it.

The rest of the game was an anti-climax. What was running compared to driving? Amity won by a smaller margin that usual, but only the scorekeeper William was sure of the details, for Leviathan had won, really won, by the spectacular appearance of the first motor car any of them had ever seen, a thing about which only a few had heard rumors, still a device of private invention and whimsical manufacture. As for Lille's sports-day cake, Perley had won it in the raffle, so although his compliments were predictable, the dish was safe.

Emmeline had seen her husband in the parsonage window, white with rage at the games of Sodom and Gomorrah, at the godless chariot moved by devils instead of horses, at his own whore of a wife wearing the forbidden, the sin-colored, jacket. Though she didn't know it, his state of mind was the more vicious because his horse was limping and one of the Sick had leaned out of bed, barked "Jump!" and vomited across the ties of his black ministerial shoes. He'd jumped then, but too late. He'd kicked those shoes off before he was out of the yard, and sluiced them, standing in his stocking feet, at the town pump. He had thought to discipline his wife by ordering her to clean them, but he couldn't bear to bring vomit into the house, his house. More his than hers. His feet left damp prints. Although Emmeline lacked these details of his day, she sensed that prolonging her escape would not further domestic tranquility.

She was barely through the door when Joab leaped from the parlor, frothing, shouting "Ephesians Chapter Five Verses 22 and 23!"

Emmeline, though used to him, was a little startled. She knew the passage well: "Wives, submit yourselves unto your husbands, as unto the Lord! For the husband is head of the wife, even as Christ is the head of the church." And knowing it well, she had her retort ready. She'd been saving it for some time.

"'See, I will feed thee with wormwood and give thee water of gall to drink!' Jeremiah 9:15," she said, and stuck out her tongue.

"You? Quoting scripture at me, you infidel?" he cried.

"You think they didn't teach Bible at Oak Gove, you hypocrite, you whited sepulcher?" she spat back. "It was Oak Grove Seminary once, I'll have you know!" Lord, but this was fun! Like Amity she was winning by a narrow margin, but she was winning— Wife 2, Husband 1.

"How come your feet are wet?" she added. "You go baptizing without your boots, or what?"

Dancing with rage in his wet stockings, he ripped from the wall, snapping its cord, their wedding-present copy of his favorite print, The Doctor, a sage healing the sick. He had always seen himself in it. Emmeline, still near the door, held it open in time to let that egregious piece of sentimentality fly through and crash. She'd always hated it. Home run.

CHAPTER TWELVE

About an hour before school was due to start, a pair of wound-up seventh grade boys took a shortcut through the cemetery. If they got to the schoolyard early enough they could get hold of the baseball bat before the eighth-graders got it. They reckoned they needed the practice. Lille noticed and knew them, and while some teachers would have run out and shrilled at them, she was not that teacher. She reckoned they had as much right to the graveyard as she did-- they were none of them dead—so she went back to organizing her day. Once again she'd been too ambitious and now she knew it.

The boys paused at the unmarked grave that had caught the attention of the Decoration Day women the day before. Sods had been cut with fair tidiness and re-laid, but they could see the edges. The sods looked temporary. They looked like doors that could swing open. They looked like trouble.

"Who do you think's under that there?" said Boy One.

"Dunno," said Boy Two. "Athena Crocker said it might be somebody's old dog. Nobody heard nothing about a dead dog, though, nor a funeral neither."

"Wanta look?" suggested One.

"Me? No way," said Two. "You want to pull up that grass I'll hold your stuff."

"Might be something pretty bad," One teased. "Some old dead face all rotten and its eyes all fallen in, might get right up and crawl out."

"Shut up!"

"You shut up!"

But now that the idea had come up, somebody needed to execute it. Preferably not them. And there like a gift was the bravest boy in school, the sixth-grader who'd do anything, just then scuffing down the road in a brown cloud. "Frank!" they yelled, "Frank Putnam! Come have a look at this!" And they had their ticket.

"Let's dig in!" said Frank cheerfully. "We need to peel them sods back so it don't show."

Fifteen minutes later the three bolted through the schoolroom door and flung themselves at Lille's desk, all jabbering at once. "Miss Nickerson, Miss Nickerson, it's a false grave, it's a fake, nobody's in it, there's nothing there, nobody DUG!"

"Hush," she said. "The others will be here before you know it. What do you mean, nobody's in it? I hate to ask how you know. The oldest one, tell me. You other two, be quiet." But she knew her boys, she knew it would have been Frank who got his hands dirty. She had an awful flash of Frank up to his elbows, grabbing some corpse by the neck.

"It was a mystery, you see," said the oldest boy, "and we wanted to solve it. So we peeled those sods back very careful, and the dirt wasn't even stirred up. It hadn't been dug in one bit, no rocks, no nothing, like dug dirt looks."

Lille nodded. It was well observed. She valued observation over good behavior, so they had her and they knew it.

"Look here," she said, "don't say a word to anybody right now, not your best friends or your brothers or those girls I've seen you cut your eyes at. No notes. It's our secret for now. We'll talk about it some more later. See, it's somebody else's secret first, and we don't know whose. Could be some big-time crook from down to Boston." That's not how she was betting, but she thought she might scare or thrill them into silence till she and Lib could figure out what was up. Lib knew people she didn't.

The boys didn't need to tell each other that they'd keep the secret. Why, she hadn't even scolded them for digging up a grave. She'd probably even tell them when she found out. She might need their help, even. Frank thought that in particular.

73

Lille wasn't sure why she'd shut the boys up. Turning them loose might have been as good a way as any to find out why there was apparently a false grave beside the true ones. She didn't think they were play acting. With difficulty she kept her mind on the complicated day she'd arranged.

She'd got carried away by the whole Civil War thing, that was the mess she'd landed herself in. One of the messes. She'd thought it might be a good thing for the children to do history by talking to the old soldiers while they still had them, their grandpas and great-uncles and cousins. The math had worked well enough—nine surviving soldiers, eighteen schoolchildren, but of course some old soldiers had a litter of descendants, others few or none. In the end she made a list of veterans, told the children to go in pairs, one older with one younger, and to sign up. She made sure that girls went with girls, and that they visited some old soldier reputed to keep his britches on. The younger child was to ask for a memory of being a soldier, the elder for a memory of the war's end, Appomattox or the revue in Washington where the 20th Maine had borne a distinguished role. The youngest children, first and second grade, were allowed to draw illustrations rather than write reports. And today, on this day of false graves and secrets, she had to keep her grip on revelations and memories.

She started with Hugh and Harold, who had sought permission to interview their grandfather together on the grounds of twinship, but had been granted it because Hugh could do a report as well as anyone else. "Mud!" said Harold, "Grandfather said the mud was so deep it pulled their boots right off their feet, didn't he, Hugh?" Hugh nodded and Harold held up a picture on a piece of brown paper: The bottom half was still brown, the top half colored blue for sky. A man's head in a soldier's cap balanced just above the sea of brown. The room howled with delight. Harold blushed and grinned. Lille suspected Hugh's idea, Harold's execution, but there was no sorting out twins. "He told me a lot of things," said Hugh, "but what I liked best was how nice everyone acted after the cease fire, which means everyone stop shooting. The northerners shared their food with the southerners, because they weren't enemies any more, you see, they were all just worn-out soldiers. And Grandfather said when the southerners put down their flags he saw them tear off little pieces to put in their pockets. I liked that too."

"So do I," said Lille.

And she did, but her mind was half occupied with what the three boys had found, or found the lack of, in the cemetery. She disciplined herself to listen, to admire, to understand, as the drawings and reports that she'd provoked were presented with pleasure. About the illustrated life of a soldier the school saw campfires, coffee, letters, a flag planted on a hill, something presumed to be a horse ridden by something presumed to be Chamberlain, a gun going off, something like a photograph in a frame, and lumps of spruce gum across a page like polka dots.

The grandfathers and neighbors had done well by the children and even the crabbiest of them had seemed pleased to be asked, Lille gathered. Even in the midst of her distraction she thought that between them all there had emerged a memory of the laying down of arms and the parade of winners, an actual restoration of the Union, as though the Smith twins had pounded each other and then stretched out in their common bed. It was not what some of the older boys had wanted, she could see that, and she supposed that view of it would prevail, but this generation in Leviathan at least had heard something true from people who'd been there.

At noon she wondered whether she could make some excuse to go home, she itched to consult with her brother, lately more of a support than she'd thought him previously. But no, she mustn't add irresponsibility to whatever shabby thing had already happened, though maybe it wasn't a bad thing, maybe it was just a weird thing, like sod-cutting practice. She didn't think so. Maybe it was a joke invented by the boys. She didn't think so. If she left the noon break in the hands of the oldest girls for half an hour, she'd be the shabby one. For the first time in years she really wanted somebody older—Perley and Susie, her mother, Lib's unlikely pal the lawyer—but she was the schoolteacher, she couldn't admit that. At school she was the grown-up.

"Now," she said, inventing fast when school resumed, knowing that they had to be distracted with something else new, something this population would like, something that would distract her too, "let's do some rhymes, maybe we can even write some verses on the board. Never mind groaning, you big boys. Is 'Casey at the Bat' a sissy poem? Is baseball sissy? What rhymes with 'bat'?" At once she was peppered with that easiest of rhymes, even the first graders contributing their instruction in CATS on MATS. She sowed one-syllable rhyme words as though they were garden seeds or hen feed—*sweet, free, sun, cake,* though she foresaw that she'd find poems involving "feet" and "pee," and then a gift for the older boys, *shoot* and *flag* and the real winner, *grave.* Let's see, she thought, what my diggers will do with that.

"At least four lines, please," she said, "and put your name on them. I'll take them home and enjoy them. You may work together with your seatmates, or alone, whichever you agree on." The room settled into hums and giggles. Good thing the school committee never came without tipping her off.

At the end of the day she loped home, her pockets stuffed with verses, and sought her brother. She had not stopped to examine the non-grave as she passed it: she trusted the data.

"Lib," she said, following him out to the barn, most unusual, "let me ask you a question, or maybe for an opinion."

In either case, thought Lib, *What the hell is up? She hasn't wanted my opinion since the barn cat was nursing the skunk baby. But it's not a trap, I've known her face all my life.*

"Do my best," he said, and meant it.

"Between you and me," Lille said, the words making her feel like a child again, "three of my boys said that they found a fake grave up there, sods cut and put back, no digging. Got any ideas who would have done that or why?"

"Huh," said Lib, thinking as fast as he ever had, "did Athena seem to know anything?"

"Didn't stop to talk to her, came straight home."

"Huh," said Lib again. "Okay, as you say, between you and me, I've got an idea but no proof of it. When I came back from Currans the other night, that peddler'd just fallen down Odin's ravine and broken his neck. Odin sent me for the minister, said as a selectman he'd take care of it, guy didn't have any friends or relatives they knew of. I did it and came home. Don't know why I didn't tell you, maybe Odin told me not to, and I'd been thinking about other stuff when he stopped me. Might be buried up there, unmarked, it's what I'd expect, only you say he isn't. Doesn't seem like they'd have hauled him to the dump, not very polite and it was getting pretty dark, though he did have me tell Nutter to hitch up. All I know, but I'd guess it's connected."

"So," said Lille, speaking slowly, "I suppose I could tell the Boys a stranger died and apparently the town meant to bury him there but someone must have shown up and claimed him. Hate to lie to them even that much, after they trusted me, after they all think I don't lie, but I guess it's the best I can do. Well, I'll work on it. But now I'd sure like to know where Mick the peddler went, besides straight to hell."

"So would I," said Lib, "maybe. Not to change the subject, but why are your pockets crunchy?"

"Glad to change it," she said. "I'm crunchy because I had to keep my gang busy this afternoon and made them write poetry. I haven't looked at it yet."

"Well shell it out," said Lib, "let's see some of it."

"Here's a cross little note from Millie Goss," said Lille. "I do NOT like that child. She says, *'On purpose you gave us no rymes for God or Jesus or Heaven or Saved, so it is not my fault that I have only two lines instead of four. YOU GO TO HELL IF YOU'RE A SINNER/ BUT I AND JESUS ARE HAVING DINNER.'* Insufferable brat."

Lib whistled. "How have you not killed her?" he said. "What else you got?"

"Frank Putnam's," Lille said, having ferreted in her pocket. "He was, of course, one of the boys involved with the fake grave. Here it is: 'Bring me a shovel or bring me a spade/Nobody says a Putnam's afraid/ And of all the Putnams, Frank is the boldest,/ Though he isn't the youngest nor isn't the oldest.' May well be the funniest, though. I kind of love that boy. Got my eye on him."

"I think I can stand one more," Lib said, "for now."

Lille ferreted again. "Oh dear, it's that poor Gladys Wayne's. She's got some spunk, though, and she likes geography. Let's see: 'In China they eat ris'-- that's r-i-s, which I'm pretty sure means rice. She's only seven, and when you think of her parents--."

"Don't chatter," said Lib, "just read it."

Lille raised an eyebrow. "'In China they eat ris/ I learn the world is nice/ In France they eat sooflay/ I plan to go away.'"

They were both silent for a few moments.

"I like my job," said Lille.

Meanwhile, behind drawn curtains in the daytime or pacing beside the lake after dark, the wild-haired Joab Nutter , once respected (as he wrongly supposed), still officially the town's ecclesiastical leader, was warring with himself and his wife and his God. He was too fundamentalist to think of the grievances he thumbed as some kind of dark rosary, too proud to imagine that his agonies were merely grievances or could be counted. By now he thought of the sore places in this life as his Persecutions, for which he expected one day to wear literal stars in a heavenly crown, and wearing it to be embraced by Peter and sympathized with by Paul.

His cold-hearted wife did not appreciate him, did not understand that he was a man of substance in this life and the next. She whined for cities, hated the town where God had sent him. She no longer performed her wifely obligations at bed or board. Once she had cooked the dishes he preferred though she did not, later only the things they both enjoyed, but now she was preparing fish for dinner, fish from the lake, and he could not stomach it, could not even sit at table with it. The lake! "Jesus ate fish," she said and smiled a venomous smile.

He had lowered himself to collude with such sinners as the unclean Ruby Wayne and the half-mad Odin Crocker. Now he was in their grasp, they eyed him as though they knew him, Ruby had winked. He had meant the great Leviathan to be an ornament for his church, a marvel for his Sunday School, Leviathan himself whom God had made for the sport of it. The children would worship him then. He feared the deep waters of Grand Lake, but soon God would justify him and he would walk on the waves.

He was aware from time to time that his mind had clouded, that he was groping his way back to a memory of someone for whom he should substitute himself. But did not want to.

It was Odin's night to check on the line. For the first time he was kind of glad to be short—not so much of him to stick up as he edged over to the rope. He had put on a dark shirt and brought an old peavey handle for a poking tool in case something needed to be sounded. Sounded, a nautical word.

The tension of the rope had not changed but it felt good in his hand. There were some bushes between him and the road, so he sat down to enjoy the quiet, and the breeze off the lake that held the mosquitoes back. Athena was a good wife, but between her and the coon there was a damned lot of chittering and chattering around his place. Sometimes he got a little short with her, but not often, because she had some kind of a temper, and Junior stood up for her too. He thought about what he could buy her if he got some money from catching Leviathan. A new cook stove. A pair of rocking chairs for the porch. Maybe go out to Houlton and have dinner in the Snell House and stay overnight too. Athena could buy a new hat for church, fancy, and maybe they'd have their pictures took. Himself, he'd always thought he'd like to have a trumpet.

CHAPTER THIRTEEN

"How bad off you think he is?" said Ruby.

They were all looking in the direction of the parsonage, though it was hidden by the church. It was a question for Odin.

"Pretty bad, I reckon," said Odin, "though it's hard to tell with a minister, they're kinda queer anyhow."

"I wish to hell he'd quit going on about the rapture," said a farmer who was giving himself a small outing though the store was shut on Sundays. "I don't want to get no snatched up in the sky, rain and geese and stuff. You anxious to go, Odin?"

"Don't know if I will go," Odin said. "Might be the guy sitting in the dirt in the potato field." He sounded casual, but Ruby, who knew some reasons Odin might not be entirely confident, looked at him hard. He admired Odin, on account of his voyage and the sighting of the serpent, or as Odin sometimes said, the Beast. He looked up to him as a leader.

"What about my wife," said Ruby, "and my daughter? Can't hardly be leaving them, can I now." One of the vets wondered whether Ruby was arguing with God about the Rapture plan, or what. There wasn't a person there who didn't think that Edna Mabel would be better off without him, and when had he given a rat's ass about his kid. One or two were amazed that Ruby Wayne imagined he might get a pass to heaven, though they could see that he'd prefer being raptured to the labor of climbing Jacob's ladder. Ruby waved his hand around his ears and slapped his head once or twice. Noseeums, he thought, but nobody else seemed to be troubled.

Everyone was pleased to have a visiting minister to the pulpit. Change was ever welcome, especially change from Joab Nutter, who was supposed to be out of town but who had reliably been reported peering from behind his wife's curtains. "Having a breakdown," said the older women with relish, and hadn't they just seen it coming. And now here was this retired man from Houlton, already reassuring with his ordinary suit and his calm, sane eyes.

"Good morning, my Brothers and Sisters in Christ," he said as though he heard his own words and meant them. "I have recently retired to Houlton to be near my family and breathe the clean air of the north. It is a privilege to fill in this Sunday for Mr. Nutter. I wish to speak to you about angels."

Lille and Lib exchanged a glance, as was their habit at church. They were Baptists, it being the only game in town, and although angels came up in the conversation from time to time, they did not arrive with much information attached. Angels were a phenomenon, largely, of Christmas and Easter. This fellow seemed promising, their eyes told each other.

"Do not think of angels as the state of your departed relatives," the preacher admonished, "for although we believe that they are happy in Heaven, having been good people and believers, angels, real angels, are a different order of created being, who live on other planes and know in other ways, and although the Bible, the source of our knowledge, does not itself say what I am about to tell you, tradition and the studies of a very early Christian have described for us nine kinds of angels: the fiery Seraphim, the six-winged Cherubim, the all-seeing Thrones; the great middle ranks of Dominions, Virtues, and Powers; and at the bottom—the bottom!— the ones more familiar to us, the Archangels like Gabriel who will blow the trumpet at the end of the world, like the warrior Michael who contended with Satan and threw him from Heaven. And even the regular Angels whom we sometimes see, the errand-runners of the glorious ranks, are so vivid and flaming that the first thing they said to the shepherds in the fields was 'Be not afraid!' And we know that shepherds are no cowards."

Lib and Lille were enchanted by the sweep of his oratory, and indeed pleased glances were general around the church. This was new material, a new way of putting it, stimulating but not not threatening, though there were some small pockets of stubbornness re the angelic state of the departed. There was a sense of a congregation settling back against wooden pews. The children were a little hesitant, they'd been burned more than once, but they snuggled into the fullness of their mothers' skirts or pressed against their fathers. Some thumbs sneaked into mouths and were pulled out gently and wiped on handkerchiefs.

"Angels," the calm voice went on, "ministered to our Old Testament forbears quite often, as you will recall. Remember the angels who came to Abraham and Sarah to announce that Sarah would give birth at the age of 90, and how she laughed? I always liked that in Sarah, didn't you? But it wasn't terribly polite. And angels came to rescue Abraham's nephew Lot from the fires of Sodom, but the wicked townspeople attempted to lay hands of them for impure purposes."

"What are impure purposes?" someone's child asked audibly.

"Shoveling manure," said a deep voice. *Well of course,* thought most of the children and a few of the adults, *you wouldn't make the company shovel out behind the cows.*

Lille's shoulders shook. That man should have been a teacher, he was fast on the draw.

"Angels, you see," the visiting minister resumed, "and this is the point, do not always come with wings and celestial fire. No, they can look like ordinary men. Therefore Paul says to us in his letter to the Hebrews, Chapter 13, Verse 2, 'Be not forgetful to entertain strangers: for thereby some have entertained angels unawares.' They come to earth wearing bodies like ours as perhaps we shall go to Heaven wearing bodies like theirs, but we will not be angels, we will be humans in glorious dress. I hope they let us use the wings, don't you? I sometimes dream of flying above Houlton, you know, gazing down at the roof of the Opera House and all the horses and rigs in Market Square.

"Now that said, my children (and we are all God's children, which is why you're my brothers and sisters), what a shock it would be to find that we'd been rude to an angel! I think we'd be looking up to the clouds for more than lightning then, would we not?"

"The Lightning is a yellow Fork / From Tables in the sky," Lib said in his head. It was his favorite Dickinson poem, a secret treasure. The fork-droppers were presumably angels, having a good meal at home with no shoveling. He smiled.

"Therefore we must bear in mind," said the minister, "that any stranger, any stranger at all, may be an angel and not look it. For angels, you know, are everywhere in their coming and going. There is a poet still alive in England who wrote a moving poem about the ubiquity of angels—ubiquity, meaning everywhere-ness. Here's what he said, 'The angels keep their ancient places:--/Turn but a stone and start a wing!/ 'Tis ye, 'tis your estranged faces,/That miss the many-splendored thing.' The poet's name is Francis Thompson, and though he is a great sufferer he knows his angels. We miss the splendor, you see, we overlook the angels, so we must treat strangers as if we at least recognize the possibility. For, says Paul, some have entertained angels unawares!"

Here Athena looked sideways at Odin, who ignored it. Whatever disguised angels might do to, or for, or with, humans, he reckoned, they absolutely did not chuck rocks at raccoons.

Lib wondered whether that poem was in print, and whether the Currans would have it.

"But that is not the worst of it," the minister went on with unexpected stamina. The sermon was a good one, and Baptists endure, but the Hebrews repetition had sounded as though it might be a closing shot. Oh well. The children were dozing off, which beat either of their responses to Nutter. "Suppose we miss not only the angels but our Lord Jesus Christ himself? For he warns us in the 25th Chapter of Matthew that at the Last Judgement, when he tells us that we gave him no food or drink or comfort, we will say in amazement, 'When saw we thee an hungered, or athirst, or sick, or in prison?' But you see, he will, like his angels, have come in disguise: he will have come as the poor and the needy, the sick and the unattractive, the bad-smelling and the ill-mannered, the utterly unlovable—as he says in Matthew, 'the least of these my brethren.' So in conclusion, dear friends, watch and pray, for the beggar at your door may be an angel or indeed Our Lord himself! Amen."

"Oh my!" said a woman on the other side of Lib, "I always thought 'the least of these' meant the children!"

"Well," said her crabby neighbor on her far side, "they can be disgusting enough to qualify, at least if they're not your own."

"You got that one nailed, Lille," Lib whispered. "Always appears like you really do care about those little grubs in your schoolhouse."

Lille just smiled. Her brother had no idea how she loved them. Most of them.

When Lib and Lille got home their mother was up and sitting in her Morris chair with a wrapper on. "Feeling pretty well today," she said. "Hired girl helped me into my chair before she left, and we've got enough cake from yesterday to gossip over. Now tell me what that lunatic of a minister was up to."

Lille put on the kettle and got the teapot out. "The amazing Mr. Nutter," she said, "appears to be hiding out behind the parsonage curtains and having an attack of the willies. What can he possibly have been up to? We had a guest preacher from Houlton."

"Well!" said Clara, "the world comes to Leviathan. Say anything interesting?"

"I'm afraid it's very grave for you, Mother," said Lib, to their surprise. It was his habit to let Lille tell the church gossip, but he'd been thinking of this joke all the way home.

"I was afraid of it," said Clara, amused already.

"It was the best preacher we've had in many a long year," said Lille. "Knew a lot of serious words, like ubiquity."

"If the schoolmarm will shut her yap," said Lib, "this one is mine."

There was a tipsy feeling of family that they hadn't known since they'd been reduced to three-fifths of themselves, sister and father gone, though they'd made sure to have laughs enough because that was who they were and they were sticking to it.

"Mother," Lib repeated, "the preacher made it plain that we must be kind and hospitable to all strangers and other pathetic folks, from the probability that they may be angels in disguise, or even Jesus himself. So I'm very much afraid that the next time some nasty peddler waters the holly hocks under your window you will have to ask him in for cake."

When they stopped howling, Lille bowed low to Lib, and Clara stood up and raised one fist. "When he comes I'll sort him out!" she said. "Just put my Bible handy and pass me my skunk!"

It's the words, Lib thought, *and the Currans. I don't know but what I'm growing up.*

The whiskered vet, who had been called Everett when he was a boy, sat taking his turn at the edge of the lake with his hand on the shaggy neck of his dog Tim. Silent together, they gazed sometimes at the water and sometimes at the moon. The rope showed no signs of activity or added weight, but the bait weighed on his mind. Back when his life had human connections -- parents, a brother, a wife—he'd felt more solidarity with his species. He wouldn't have used another human for bait then, he thought. Fish bait was probably no worse than worm food, if it came to that, and the peddler had earned no respect from his fellow men, but they would have been higher minded to offer it, maybe. The damn near unforgiveable thing he, Everett, had done, was using another man's private parts for a practical joke, to make Ruby jump. He'd used that dead penis like a Halloween bogey. He'd used the memory of his fellow soldiers dead on the field of battle to inspire the prank. He kind of wished he hadn't done that. But even more he wished his brother was alive and had done it with him. The dog leaned into his shoulder.

CHAPTER FOURTEEN

"There's that fool of a peddler," Perley said to Susie, "first time I've seen him this spring. Been wanting any shoddy goods or shall we go inside before he sees us? Goodness, what's the matter with the rabbit? Oliver?"

Oliver Twist was heading for under the bed at top speed. He thought he might scream, but he remembered that rabbits scream only when they're caught by predators, so it might not be fitting. He hoped. He knew the peddler had broken his neck and been carried away in the night. The peddler was dead! And Perley had just said there he was! He had no words for the walking dead, so he screamed *DANGER! DANGER!* in his mind with such resonance that the other animals felt it and shared his panic. MacDuff plowed headfirst into the bed covers and wrapped around Clara's feet, the cats ran for the house; Junior, who had most reason to fear the peddler revenant, having danced on his dead face, climbed the back of Athena's skirt as she stood at the sink, and anchored on her crossed apron straps. Like Oliver she screamed a little, but Junior had foreseen that and got a grip.

Athena knew much but didn't know everything. She had peeped at the peddler's exit behind Nutter's horse, though Odin likely didn't know she'd seen it. She suspected from the fake grave that they'd rolled the dead peddler into the town dump and let the crows and bobcats have him. Why not, she'd thought, if they can stomach that piece of strolling fertilizer, let them have a banquet. He'd always been mean to Junior, and if she'd had human kids he'd have been mean to them. She'd had no use for him.

Athena was excitable but not hysterical. When Junior steered her to the window and she first saw the peddler walk past, this time pushing his usual cart instead of wearing a pack basket, she felt a chill like none she'd ever known, a thing of organ and marrow. Her scalp prickled too, but under it she had a better brain than many, because it was quick. She saw the options almost at once: one of three things. First, Mick the Peddler had somehow come back from the dump, not having been dead after all, and would likely take revenge. Second and much worse, Mick the Peddler had come back from the dead and was a kind of creature beyond her naming, and he would certainly destroy Odin and his cronies, perhaps all of Leviathan, or Aroostook, or Maine. Third, and she could see the superior logic of this possibility, there were two peddlers. The one who had died had not after all been Mick, just another sleazy fake blind man with nasty goods, the kind who crawled all over thin settlements like Leviathan in summer, and they'd only seen him in the dark, not to mention that Junior appeared to have jumped on his face some. This one was the real Mick, because he had the usual cart.

"It's okay," she said in Junior's ear, "this isn't the dead guy, but you go hide if you need to."

"Mick!" she called, raising the window, "Mick!"

Junior let himself down cellar, but he kept the door cracked. He'd kill to save Athena if he had to.

The peddler turned. Crabby. Sour. Sure looked like Mick.

"I'm about out of pencils," Athena said. "And I could use a composition book if you've got one."

"Might have," the peddler said grudgingly, rummaging in his cart. "Spose you're writing down some lies. Ain't that damn coon of yours dead yet?"

"A novel, you mean?" said Athena, cancelling with his coon question any chance he had of a cookie or even a cup of water. "You never know, do you." It was Mick for sure. The other one, the dead one, had been someone else, also nasty. "You don't have a brother, do you," she said as she handed him the coins and took the writing tools.

He didn't deign to answer, just marched up to road to the Nickerson place. Slut hadn't even offered him a turn at the pump. He'd steal one at the Nickersons, they could like it or not.

"Hold up going home a minute, would you," Clara said to the hired girl, who was just leaving. "Look at how all the cats are coming in the cat door, and MacDuff's already dug under the covers. Something unpleasant must be pretty near, storm maybe or some big critter. Maybe you'd just hook that door shut. Leroy'll take care of the barn."

The girl squeaked but she did it. Life on the edge of the woods, wild but not bucolic, had trained her to hold it together.

She looked out the front parlor window. "Looks like it's just that mean old peddler," she reported, "guess that's reason enough for the animals to clear out. He threw a stick at a kitten at Ma's place, he ain't blind a bit, but good thing he missed, we'd a taken him down like a pack of wolves. We like kittens, at Ma's house."

"Here too," said Clara. "He moved on yet?"

"He's pumping hisself a drink," said the girl. "I'll be sure to wash out the cup when he leaves."

"Good," said Clara. "Hot water and soap?"

"Got anything stronger?" said the girl.

"You're a good girl, Lois," said Clara. "Help yourself to a cookie while you wait. Wonder why the animals got so upset."

The animals, already alerted by Oliver's panic and some chittering from next door, had no desire to see whatever it was. They had known curiosity to work out badly.

"I guess I'll just go see what ails that rabbit," Perley said, and patted Susie's shoulder, holding it for a moment to deflect any (possibly not ill founded) accusation that he loved Oliver more than he did her. She wasn't snarky about it, there was no snark in her nature, but once he'd actually heard a touch of wistfulness. The truth, he thought, following Oliver Twist upstairs, was that the rabbit had done something more like filling in for his child, his daughter who taught in Bangor and was friendly with them but had another life now. Or maybe Oliver was more of a goofy son who couldn't leave home. Either way, he sure enough loved him. With some stiffness Perley stretched out on the hooked rug and laid his cheek to the floor, glad it wasn't winter.

"Oliver, sweetheart, what's the matter?" he said softly, reckoning that rabbits don't respond well to a bracing tone. Oliver was in a ball with his eyes clenched. "You want to come out here and let me hold you?"

Oliver in fact wanted it very much, but he was afraid to move. The Bad Thing might hear the motion. He wished Perley would get under the bed with him. Perley knew it and tried, thanking Susie for being such a good housekeeper. He'd say it out loud when he went back downstairs, he thought, and she'd be pleased. He got one arm and his shoulder under the bed rail, enough to reach the rabbit with his finger tips and stroke him. Oliver Twist sidled a little farther in his true love's direction. He might be safe even from the Bad Thing with Perley's whole hand on him. "We'll make biscuits later," Perley said, and they both sighed and briefly napped.

When they woke up again, Susie was lying on the floor at the other side of the bed. "You boys may be crazy but you're still mine," she said. "Find any dust?"

Lib was at the Curran camp again. He hadn't told his mother or Lille that he was trying to get himself some education, but he thought his mother knew it. She'd never tried to get in the way of it. Not that Lille would either, but she might make jokes.

They'd had pie and were talking casually. Lib had just borrowed Mr. Thoreau's account of hiking around the north woods, places Lib knew, some of them. He'd never thought of people bothering; he felt more connected to the world outside every day, though Leviathan suited him fine, he wasn't restless like Lille. He'd slip the book into his room. He read at night now by the kerosene lamp. They must suspect. Someday soon he'd read downstairs with his mother and Lille instead of letting on to play solitaire, or cribbage with the hired man.

"Eileen's been teasing for a cat," her mother said. "She's about stopped sneezing around cats now, but we're not sure she's stopped for good. We might borrow one for a couple of days if we can arrange it."

"Do you have cats?" Eileen asked Lib. "Do you make carvings of them?"

"I could, I guess," said Lib, "though I never did yet. Yes, we have three or four cats that catch mice for us in the barn and come inside when they want to. I imagine you could borrow one of those. They're nice and tame, and if they weren't happy here they'd just walk home, but if you feed them as well as you feed me they'd likely take to the experiment. But you know what else we've got? We've got a skunk!"

Sensation.

"Really? You mean in the house?" said Mrs. Curran.

"And it hasn't sprayed?" said the lawyer.

"Ooh," said Eileen, "maybe I wouldn't sneeze around a skunk!"

"You'd sneeze if it sprayed!" her father said.

Lib was tickled to have surprised them the way they'd so often surprised him. He explained once again about the skunk kit suckled by the barn cat, about its sweet nature and affection for his mother, about how it kept her company in bed. Eileen laughed with delight.

"Could I see it sometime?" she said.

Lib looked at her parents. He hadn't meant to start anything. "Maybe when you folks are out for a walk some evening you'd like to stop by the house and I'd bring MacDuff, that's his name, onto the screen porch? Mother can get out of bed more and more, so she might come out too, and that would keep the skunk real happy."

Their faces said possibly but not for certain, don't want to intrude, not for certain but coming around. Eileen, who could read them, relaxed.

"You know," Lib said, "the two houses before ours have special animals too. I don't know if you've been introduced to the neighbors, but you can see them from here."

"We know Perley and Susie Junkins," said the lawyer. "We stopped to see Perley once about some selectman business. I believe there was a rabbit."

"Yes, fine big rabbit called Oliver Twist," said Lib, "and Susie says she thinks Perley loves that rabbit more than he loves her, but she's joking. I think. They make real good pets. The house between them and us is a little wilder but they're solid neighbors and guess what they've got—a coon. You get a sweet one they make good pets too. We all love furry animals on Haney Brook Road."

The lawyer caught Lib's eye on "furry." There'd been just a momentary hitch before it. He remembered that Odin Crocker, one of the good people in the middle house, was bent with his gang of idle dreamers on catching, killing, and preserving the fabled Creature of East Grand Lake. Too bad Lib would never get to law school, he thought. "Well, I guess we can at least manage the skunk and the rabbit someday," he said. "We'll trade our literary lessons for your nature lessons, Lib, how's that?"

That's how Lib went home mid-day on such a pedagogical cloud—he, who had hardly begun to learn, knowing something to teach!—that he was hardly even startled at hearing Athena shout, "Odin, you damn fool, how do you know you didn't throw an angel into the town dump unawares?"

CHAPTER FIFTEEN

Odin had strolled home on towards noon and found a wild-eyed wife, a coon with the heebie-jeebies, and no smells of cooking.

"Anything wrong with the stove?" he said. It wasn't sarcasm so much as an oblique expression of concern. By asking about the stove he was asking about her, and Junior too; Athena knew it, but she wasn't having it.

"You'll get bread and butter and pickles if you're lucky!" she said and wept, but soon pulled herself together. Her upbringing hadn't favored weakness.

"Sit down, Odin," she said, "and tell me the truth about what you and those other fools did with that dead man. You and that trashy Ruby and that raving minister."

Odin sat down but Athena was up and pacing so he stood up again too. "What do you mean?" he blustered, and reached for the sour pickles.

"I couldn't sleep," said Athena, "and now I don't know as I'll ever sleep again. I mean I saw you haul off that dead man, the three of you and old whisker-face too, and I think you took him to the dump and let on to make a grave, because you couldn't bother to be decent. And the minister in on it? I always knew he was no good, him in his beetle-ass jacket, but this beats all. What'd he do, say some words out there over the garbage and the busted chairs and Ruby's dead cat?"

"Spose we did, and I ain't saying it's so, it was just that nasty Mick the peddler that always shied rocks at Junior, so what would you care if we had?"

"Number one, surprise, that wasn't Mick. He came through today, mean as ever. Oh don't turn white, you got more sense than that. The other guy's still dead, whoever he was, UNLESS he wasn't a human at all, by the way. Remember that substitute's sermon, how angels come looking like humans and we're good to them or we ain't, and we don't want to make a mistake? Odin, you damn fool, how'd you know you didn't throw an angel into the dump unawares? Like that minister said? How you think our lives gonna go then? Blessings from above? I don't think so. We've always made out all right, till now, but what if that's over?"

Odin leaned his head on his hands. He was sitting down again. "Okay," he said, "we're married, right. We took vows to stick with each other through bad and good and richer and poorer and all that. Well what if I was trying to make us richer, right, and I had to do some stuff. You don't know the whole of it. You got to keep this a secret forever, you swear?"

"I swear," Athena said, because she couldn't see any other way. She'd just remembered the other thing the minister said, about Jesus coming to call wrapped in really disgusting people, and you had to treat him right too, or hear about it at the Judgement. She'd begun to shake.

"We didn't put the dead guy in the dump, dammit. We took him down to the lake and baited that great big hook we'd had made. Took four of us to get the barbs into him and it was some nasty. Feel sick thinking about it, kinda, but there it is, we done it."

For the first time in her life Athena thought she might faint. It appeared she was married to a fool who'd use Jesus for fishing bait, and there was no special place to go if she left him. She put her forehead on the table and felt a very small dry hand reach up and hold her finger.

When she felt stronger again, she thought with amazement of Joab Nutter. He must have lost his mind. Anyhow, she'd rather be married to Odin than to him. She'd most rather be married to Ruby Wayne than to him, provided she didn't take fits. She'd never thought much of Nutter's wife either, uppity little piece, but she guessed she owed something to her as one woman to another. Emmeline, for the love of God. She might have brains enough to get out before he cracked completely, wedding vows be damned.

She hung up her apron and set off by way of the road. She didn't want to mess with the cemetery or the church, either one. The parsonage had its curtains drawn, not very hospitable. She almost turned back, but instead she rapped on the kitchen door. This was not a formal call.

"Your husband home?" Athena asked, without ceremony.

"No, he's not," said Emmeline Nutter, and started to shut the door. She looked hard as a hazelnut.

"Good enough," said Athena, and put her foot in the opening. "I don't want him to hear what I got to tell you." She was no buttercup herself.

They took each other's measure and calmed down.

"Lookit," said Athena, "this is what you'd call confidential. My man and yours and some other fool men who ought to known better, they got mixed up in some nasty business together. I'm sworn not to tell, but wife to wife I kinda owe you. Alls I can say is if it's handy for you to go visit family somewhere this might be the time to do it."

"Had my valise packed for a month," Emmeline said. "I can see there's something ugly wrong with him, and I wouldn't mind being gone before it gets loose. Don't know why I ever married a crazy man."

"Well you've kept to yourself!" said Athena. "I think we coulda been pretty good friends, if we'd been smart enough to know it. Too late now, I guess. You better make a run for it. Can you harness up and drive?"

"I love to," said Emmeline, "I'm good at it, and Joab never let me if he could help it. I'll take that light rig he bought for his pastoral calls and leave him the wagon, no horse of course, but I have a feeling his life here's over. I can make it to Houlton before it's real dark if I start now, put up in a hotel, let the livery station sell the horse and rig, and tomorrow I'm on the train to Bangor. I've got friends in Portland. Always fancied Boston too. Want to leave Odin and come along?"

"Guess not," said Athena, "but thank you truly. I'm kinda interested in how it all works out here, and Odin's not much but I'm used to him. Then there's the raccoon. I don't believe he'd care for the city. You be happy, Emmeline Nutter, and if you want to know the end of the story you got my address." She turned and walked away from a woman she might have had some fun and solace with, if their husbands hadn't both been jerks. But, compared to Joab, Odin still looked pretty good.

Odin was thinking that maybe somebody should let Ruby know that he might be running into Mick the Peddler. Ruby was pretty excitable. But he was too late. While he debated between looking for Ruby at the store or hitching up to drive to Ruby's place, and which was harder, walking there or driving, the peddler turned into Ruby's scrap of a dooryard and nestled his ass among the roots of a tree. He'd been rained on somewhere, it appeared, or maybe pumped water on his head, and was unfortunately pretty wet, so when Gladys told her dad that the peddler was outside and wanted to see him, and Ruby got a description that seemed to confirm his worst fears, he passed out cold for the first time in his life that didn't involve drinking. Fortunately his wife was there and knew what to do, but he opened his eyes just as she drew back to land him a kick in the ribs.

"Gladys," he said, "does that peddler have any pants on?" She was laughing too hard to answer him, but what he was thinking was that even if Mick had come alive and got unhooked and crawled out of the lake, he'd have been stark naked; his clothes had been jammed into a feed sack and heaved as far into the woods as Ruby had been able to throw it, after all that work.

The third of the conspirators, Joab Nutter, came back to a black house in a black world. He'd been pacing the roads when the sun went down and he'd fully expected, had every right to expect, that his wife would have lighted the household lamps when twilight set in and she could still find the matches. He saw lights enough in the windows of other people, luckier people, to estimate where his house must be and head for it. He stumbled now and then. There was a moon, but clouds kept hiding it, and a few stars, the things he'd once assumed he'd be wearing on his brow in heaven. When he'd been sure of his prestige in heaven. Been sure there was one, even. He was pretty sure about hell, and his slattern of a wife would go to it, he reckoned. Him, he was apparently in it already.

He laid his hand on his front door, found it unlatched. Went in. Hand to the wall he groped down the hall to the kitchen, where the matches ought to be. It was black as his wife's velvet dress that he forbade her to wear in Leviathan. "I'll not have my wife looking like a Magdalen," he'd told her firmly, authoritatively. She had walked away, her fists clenched. What if some fist, or some claw, should shoot out of the parlor as he passed its door? What if some beast should leap? What if it had teeth to tear him? He hurried, stumbled a little, put his hand on something that moved—no, it was only his own Sunday gloves on the hall table.

In the kitchen there was at least a window, a patch of gray. He blessed God for it. He had never known how much he feared the dark. He had presumed himself master of it. The most portable of the lamps was on the kitchen table where it belonged, the matches beside it. Should he forgive her, then? At most, only for the unlighted house. Probably not even for that. Where was she, out gallivanting? But he'd seen to it that she had no friends. Was some disgusting neighbor ill? He struck three matches before his hand steadied enough to bring one to the wick. It took. He put the chimney back over it and turned up the flame. Fiat Lux, he said to himself, Let There Be Light. But look, a note on the table.

"Joab," it said, "Whatever dark business you've gotten into, I want no part of it. I have taken the horse. He never liked you. Emmeline."

He tore it with his teeth and spat it down the lamp chimney. Fiat Nox, then. Let There Be Night again and forever.

It was his turn to check the tension of the rope, but he didn't remember it until later. Eileen, who often watched the line from her bedroom window if she was wakeful, saw with admiration that he was shinnying down it—going to check the hook up close, she supposed, which seemed to her pretty smart. But soon her mother came and tucked her in again, so she lost any chance to see him come back up.

CHAPTER SIXTEEN

It was still light after dinner as the three Nickersons sat around the table. Three not counting the animals, that is. MacDuff knew that Oliver and Junior sometimes sat on the tables at their houses, and ate things too. He wasn't sure how he felt about that. A table top is pretty high up and formal if you come from a line of burrow dwellers. He'd always settled for under the table, even if it was the kitchen table, even if they'd been shelling peas, say, and had covered the top with newspapers, fine for animals to sit on, but now somehow he needed to prove himself. He'd gone out in a boat with Lib once, that was brave, but it wasn't high up. So he turned to Clara, his best human, and looked at the top of it. Lib put him in Clara's arms, and Clara set him gently on the table, and the cat who'd mothered him hopped up to keep him company. He liked it pretty well if he didn't get too near the edge. He and the cat had some chicken off the platter.

"Father brought over a load of rotted manure for the garden today," Lib remarked.

"Ah," said Clara, "Manfred always was romantic."

Lille laughed. "You know what my earliest memory of Father is? Sitting there at the desk and shuffling cards so they flew together. I still think that someday I'll learn to do that."

"I know how," said Lib unexpectedly. "I'll show you."

Lille threw him a look of warmth. He caught it.

"What was Father like when you first knew him, Mother?" Lille said, "If you don't mind my asking."

"Good looking in a dark, bad-boy way. Smarter than a lot of the boys, didn't smell like the barnyard either. I could have done better with a broader field of endeavor, but we didn't get far from Leviathan and my sisters seemed to like being married. So there we were. It wasn't a great romance but he was kind of fun. He's a hard worker too. He'd rather chop wood than go fishing. Don't know where you got your boat thing from, Lib."

Gift from God, Lib thought, but he didn't say it. "Oh," he said instead, and changed the subject: "Father said there was a lot of gossip about the Nutters," he said. "Either of you hear anything?"

"Athena called me in and said his wife had run off," said Lille, "and I had an idea she might know more than she thought she ought to tell."

MacDuff thought, *Oliver thumped a good bit last night. Maybe Susie saw the Nutter woman run off. I wonder how fast she can run. More than likely one of the humans will come around in a day or two and tell it all. Funny things they enjoy. I think I've been up here enough.* He clicked across to Clara and bumped his head against her bosom.

"You're welcome for the chicken," she said, "you want to get down now?"

Lap, he thought at her, and she heard him. In a moment she was holding him and rubbing his chin. He loved her.

"Back to the gossip," said Clara, "what did you think Athena was not saying, Lille, you who see through things better than most?"

Lille was pleased. It was true, and yet she hadn't been sure her mother knew that about her. It had sometimes of course been handy if she didn't. But in the new configuration and re-shaping of the Nickerson family, everyone grown up, it could be fun, it could be honest.

"I think she knows for sure that Mrs. Nutter ran off, and I think she knows why. And I think she might have helped. But what I want to know worse is what's become of her crazy husband. Did he run off with her? I don't think so. There'd be nobody for the pair to run from except the town, and I can see why they might want to, but all they'd have to do is tender a resignation and load up the wagon. And nobody's seen him for a few days, apparently."

Lib hung his head a bit in the old way. "Somebody might have."

"Oh Lord," said Clara, "the lake. Your summer friends saw something, didn't they? Oh tell me he didn't go into the lake. I don't like the man, never saw him but once and couldn't stand him then, but he's been a fine entertainment for me on Sunday afternoons."

"Dunno," said Lib, "but good lawyers don't jump to conclusions, and the Currans said they saw something queer the other night, somebody messing with that big rope Odin tied to a tree-- fishing for Leviathan everyone says, just like him. Couldn't see the person too well, he was all in black and there were clouds across the moon, but now and then there'd be some light to show how the water went on being troubled around the rope. They were glad they'd put Eileen to bed. She likes to watch the rope when she's bored, just in case she catches the moment when the big serpent comes up. She knows he's not real, though."

"More than Odin knows, then," said Clara. "Athena's always been about ten times as smart as he is. Why will women do that!"

"No wonder she keeps a coon for company," Lille said.

MacDuff, who'd been listening, was shocked. If that was true of Junior, could it be that he himself was just filling in for the one they called Father? He looked up with anxiety but Clara soothed him.

"No, MacDuff," she said, "you're here because you're the best skunk, the cleverest skunk, the sweetest skunk in the whole County. It's Manfred who was the make-do until we could find you, I hope you know that." He did, once she'd said it.

The humans sat in an easy silence and watched the light fade. *This is the night,* Lib found himself thinking, somewhat to his surprise, *this is the night I admit to learning, to being a reader of serious things.* Still he sat until Lille got up and lighted the table lamp. She fetched her novel and her mother's. Charles Dickens. Mrs. Humphrey Ward. It was the nightly ritual.

"Guess I'll join you ladies," said Lib with a straight face. "I've been reading when I go to bed but this looks like more fun. If you don't mind."

"We'd love it," they said together, astonished, and both meant it. They waited in some suspense. They assumed he could read, of course, beyond a glance at the Houlton paper. Their slouchy, sweet Lib, who lazed in his boat or whittled! Jack London's stories, maybe? They couldn't have been much more surprised if MacDuff had pushed in a copy of *Little Lord Fauntleroy*, once a family favorite. They heard Lib's feet coming back down.

Blackwood's! The women couldn't get their minds around it for a moment as he laid it in front of his chair. Lib was reading a literary magazine, and one both famous and current! Where had he got it? What was in it that he wanted? Someone squeaked with surprise, and then all three were laughing, and Lille hugged him, which she never did.

"Yup," said Lib, "and if I'd known you'd get this excited I might have told you before. Might. Not sure. Yes, the Currans have been lending me things. She's an English teacher, or was before she married, y'know, and one day he asked me how it happened Father hadn't sent me out to Ricker and I told him the truth as well as I could—never mind, Mother, they were bad times—and he said a person could just read up and educate himself. So I been reading. They tell me what I might like, and I always have. They got my number, I guess. I been a little shy about it."

"No reason to be, Liberty," said his mother. "You're the man of the house."

Before he could blush, Lille bailed him out. "Never mind that!" she cried. "Tell me what you've read, tell me what you like!"

"Oh," said Lib, "read some Emily Dickinson poems, like the one about the lightning best. Read Mr. Thoreau's book about his walk all around the Maine woods, mountains and so on. It wasn't big news, of course, but I liked the way he said it, and I liked that he'd really done it. Read some other stuff, American mostly, the lawyer thought I should begin there. He says he's going to bring me a long one about a whale hunt, *Moby Dick,* since I like the water so much, guy down in western Massachusetts wrote it, died just a few years back. But now I'm on something foreign and it's pretty wild. Don't know that you'd care for it. It's in three parts in this magazine, one a month, this is Part

Two. It's *The Heart of Darkness* by Joseph Conrad, it happens in Africa. Scary kind of stuff, but it reads pretty."

Lille, who had a fondness for Ann Radcliffe, liked the title. "I've never read any of his writing," she admitted. "Won't you read us a little taste, Lib?"

He nearly handed it to her and told her to read to them, but he was a man, even his mother said so. He chose some sentences near where he'd left off: "Going up that river was like traveling back to the earliest beginnings of the world, when vegetation rioted on the earth and the big trees were kings. An empty stream, a great silence, an impenetrable forest. . . . .On silvery sandbanks hippos and alligator sunned themselves side by side. . . . And this stillness of life did not in the least resemble a peace."

"The man can write!" said his mother, and went to bed to think about her children.

Lib and Lille stayed up a while longer. It was a day too important to finish: with the revelation of Lib's literary education, everything had changed, all the checks and balances; wrongs had been righted.

"Let's go sit on the porch," Lib proposed. It was a soft night, warm enough and aromatic with roadside plants.

"I'll grab some cookies out of the crock," Lille said.

They sat on opposite ends of the hanging glider and swung a little, sometimes sideways.

"Okay!" said Lille, after a pause. "Rot in hell, Hattie Toothaker, you vicious child-breaking excuse for a teacher, and may the devil whip your big ass with red-hot brambles. Our Lib's got free now!"

Lib choked on his cookie, spitting crumbs, and when he could, laughed. "She was a nightmare, wasn't she," he said, not a question. "She always hated me, she thought it was me put the cow flop in her desk drawer, but it wasn't. Wish I had. That was a happy day. I can still see her stick her hand in it."

"She held you back for looking out the window," Lille said. "If she hadn't done that, Father would have had no excuse to keep you home instead of sending you to Ricker. You were just being your nature-loving self. She tried to spoil your life."

"About did it,' Lib said. "Changed it, anyway."

"Changed mine too," said Lille thoughtfully.

"But you're a schoolteacher," said Lib. "Oh."

"Just so. I got an idea then that I'd teach school and do it right, be the exact opposite of her. And I have been. I am. Every time I say a kind word to some runny-nose morsel from up back I remember the day she made John Fanjoy cry when she told him his family was no good and he'd never be worth anything either. We saw him lose heart right there, remember? You ever see him around?"

"He worked in the woods for a while. Heard he got injured. Sad life, and I always kind of thought it was her fault. I remember the day she slapped that first grader's slice of cake out of her hands and spoiled it. Spoiled the pleasure of it, what's worse. Little girl was one of that huge family rented the old Estabrook house and I don't suppose she'd ever had cake to bring before, she was so proud of it. 'Pride goeth before a fall,' that's what Hateful Hattie--remember we called her that?--said, and spit sprayed out of her mouth, I can see it. That was the worst one, for me. I had to look out the window then so nobody'd see my face. I thought I should have saved that little girl and couldn't see how."

"Remember when she knocked out that 6th grader, what was his name, with the hand bell?"

"Yup. Osgood something. Heaved it at his head and dropped him like a bad potato."

"I kind of wonder now," said Lille, "why the selectmen didn't do something about her. Because she was dangerous, she might have killed one of us."

"Or several," said Lib thoughtfully. "Kids sometimes gotta be tough to survive. You ever whack anybody?"

"Not so far," said Lille, "but Millie Goss might tilt me yet."

The cookies were gone, the moon was high, MacDuff had eased out the cat door. Time for bed.

"Lib," said Lille, "I never thought she'd blame you. I was the one put the cow flop."

CHAPTER SEVENTEEN

Frankie, the sixth-grader who would do anything, who had taken control for the seventh graders in the fake-grave episode, was feeling a little restless because the matter had not been further explored. A man of action, he took his father's favorite shovel and ran the mile or so to the cemetery without breaking a sweat. He'd just dig down a ways himself, and then he'd know more. The sods didn't come off so easily now, but his shovel was excellent. He decided that he need not dig the full width of the grave to find out whether anything interesting was there. What if somebody'd buried treasure or a pirate pistol? What about incriminating letters? What about a dead animal, even, which would have interesting bones?

Half an hour's diligent work had bagged him nothing but an empty whiskey bottle and a mole in a state of advanced decay, but both of these pleased him. He tucked them behind Isaiah Ledbetter's stone for safe keeping. If Ledbetter died as young as people always said, he ought to appreciate them. Frankie wiped his hands on his pants, leaving the shovel in the excavation, and looked around for the next thing to do. It was a warm day, he wouldn't mind some time by the lake, but it seemed like a lot of the shore belonged to summer people. And then he saw Lib Nickerson walking down Haney Brook Road and carrying in his arms the most wonderful thing, a skunk.

Lib was on his way to some moments of peace on Monument

Stream. The sky was cloudless, the air delicious, and no one needed him at home. He'd asked MacDuff if he'd like to come out in the boat again, not fishing but just riding around and looking at things, and the skunk, though a bit anxious, couldn't pass it up. Junior and Oliver might see him go by, and someone would mention to the cats where he was. Lib talked to him softly all the time he carried him, hummed a little, told him how he'd brought a treat in his pocket. MacDuff snuggled against Lib's shirt, happy, and looked around. Something was running down a hill at them. That might not be good. He gestured in Frankie's direction with his head and snuggled in closer. His wild brothers would plow right along, foot in front of foot, and plan to spray whatever the thing was when it got close enough. But as Lib had assured the Currans, MacDuff had never sprayed anybody, though sometimes he'd gone off and emptied his scent sacs for health's sake.

Frankie slowed down and spoke gently but he came on. "Oh, Mr. Nickerson!" he said. "You've got a skunk! May I touch him? Would he mind?"

Lib thought possibly MacDuff would not mind, given the sensitivity of the boy's query. "Come speak to him slowly and softly," he said, "and I bet he'll like you. Skunks don't see very far, so they learn a lot from sounds."

"O beautiful skunk," said Frankie in tones so dulcet that Lib almost spoiled the effect by laughing, "I am honored to meet you and beg to admire your white stripe. I am just a one-color boy myself, but if I might stroke your back I would remember it all my life."

MacDuff nestled a little and looked up at his admirer. "Go ahead," said Lib, "he likes you. Stroke him with your finger so he doesn't worry about being grabbed."

Frankie stroked. At least two of the three almost purred despite not being anatomically set up for it.

"I got a cookie, nicked it coming out the door. Would he like a hunk of it?" Frankie asked. "Where you two going?"

"The skunk—and I imagine he would like some cookie very much—the skunk and I are going up to Monument Stream for a little silence and peace, but he isn't very used to boats so I don't dare bring anyone else along. But first I'm going to stop and show him to some friends of mine who have a camp right ahead of us. I wouldn't be surprised if they let you go in the lake there, but not in the skinny, there's a little girl."

Frankie's eyes were wider than usual, his mouth more shut. He just nodded.

The Currans were sitting on their screen porch, gazing at the water. Odin's big rope was quiet. When Laura Curran saw Lib come around the corner with a skunk under his arm and a dusty urchin beside him she began to giggle. "Lib's brought the mountain to Mohammed," she said to her husband. "Evidently the skunk does not spray, and Eileen has a couple of gentlemen callers."

He leaned forward in his porch chair and beckoned them in, thinking it better not to make sudden noises. Lib sat down on the steps.

"We've never had a misfire and never expect to, but there's no point in pushing ourselves forward," Lib said. "The guy under my armpit is MacDuff; he's coming up Monument Stream with me—that Conrad story is really something, thank you, I keep thinking Africa!—so I didn't know but what Eileen might like to see him first. Have you tried out a cat yet? The fellow beside me is Frank Putnam, by the way, relative of Black Hawk Putnam the war hero; he came along with me in hopes of putting his feet in the lake, if I give him a reference."

Lawyer Curran, Ed to his friends, was astonished at the progress in Lib's bearing and confidence. He'd believed what he'd said about education, but he could see he'd only believed half enough. "Oh, come onto the porch, all three of you," he said. "Any friend of Lib's is a friend of mine." Lib himself was startled by the breadth of the hospitality, but Frankie was outright stunned. This was the fanciest place he'd ever been inside, even just the porch. Only MacDuff was blasé. Did he see a platter of chicken? He did not.

Eileen, instructed by her mother, tiptoed in and stood back awestruck.

"I touched him with my finger," Frank told her, "but very slow and after I talked soft."

She hadn't seen him at first. She seldom met boys, besides Lib, who was more and more a man. She was only six. It was a day of miracles. Her father nodded and she crept forward.

"How do you do, Mr. Skunk," she said. "Welcome to the Curran camp. May I come closer? May I touch you?" She didn't move until Lib consulted with MacDuff and nodded. She stroked MacDuff once on his head and stepped back, not presuming. Lib nodded. She was dizzy with beaming.

"I'm not sneezing," she said to her mother.

"There are limits," said her mother, but she smiled.

Limits? What was that about? MacDuff thought. *Were they edible?*

Lib put MacDuff gently into the boat, pushed it into the water and hopped in. "You get under the little bow deck there if you'd feel safer," Lib said, "or under my seat. I've got us a snack for later. We won't fish this time, so it's better than worms, though I did put one of those in my pocket in case you prefer it. Thanks for being so nice with the young'uns. There'll be some smooth water more or less, then some bumpy water, though the wind's behind us so it won't be bad, and then the smoothest place in the world. Remember it? We fished up there last time. This time we'll just lie back and look."

MacDuff didn't like the bumpy water much, but there were Lib's feet, not as good as Clara's but they'd do. And he was having an adventure. The sky was too far away for him to see very well, Lib was right about skunk vision, but it felt clear as pump water.

At last they arrived at Monument Stream. MacDuff remembered the smells now, and the sounds. They drifted on the surface, past the cattails at the edges, past the small leaping fish. Somewhere frogs kachunked, somewhere birds sang. Lib in his bliss almost dozed, his skunk soft between his feet. Words sang in his head, "the sea-reach of the Thames," "the luminous estuary," "the ships whose names are like jewels." MacDuff moved a little and Lib opened his eyes. "Here," he said, "we haven't had our treat," and he took a chicken sandwich out of his pocket, breaking it, giving the larger half to his striped friend, dipping him some water in a cup.

107

Even had he wanted to tell it afterwards, and he never did, he could not have described the sense of shimmer in the sky, as though something might happen. When he looked at it steadily, as steadily as he could, the blue shifted to gold and yet was blue, a blue of more value. He looked at it and thought of sunrise on Monument, once when he'd crept away early. MacDuff thought of the light in Clara's eyes when they touched noses. But the Something that was there, and part of it, knew gold to be the color of Eternity. An angel, Lib perceived at once—low on the angel chain, he recalled from the sermon, and he was glad to see nothing higher. He could hardly breathe as it was. The angel paused there in its passing, congenial, balanced on its vibrations and smiling, outside all gender. "I am the Angel Leviathan," it said, "not town, not serpent-- Angel. Heaven loves you, Liberty Nickerson--you who feed your brother skunk (whom also we cherish) before yourself, and give him cool water: no one before you ever loved this quiet stream as much as its Maker intended. MacDuff, you fine skunk, dwell in joy." The sky was sky again.

What had MacDuff felt or heard? He stood with his paws on an oarlock, face turned up. He had no words to tell his friends, but he always felt that Oliver had caught a whiff of it. And Lib, even in moments when he didn't believe he'd seen it, fed off it. He was not a left-behind boy, he was a man of whom Heaven approved.

Frank and Eileen had spent a congenial afternoon in spite of their difference in ages. They had information to share, and their feet side by side in the water seemed comic.

"Want to know what that big rope is, going under the water," Eileen asked, breaking the shyness.

"I was wondering," said Frank. "What's on the other end?"

"Well," said his small informant, "I don't know for sure, but I think it must be a giant hook. There's a man with an O name who thinks he can catch a lake monster, but Father says there isn't one."

"He says that? A lot of people believe in it, though."

"Well," said Eileen, "he is a lawyer and I think they are usually right."

———

108

"A lawyer? Is that why you're rich? Only rich people have a house and a summer camp both."

"Then we must be rich, I guess. He wasn't always. He was old and poor when he went to high school, he always says so."

"So I could be a lawyer too, rich and usually right," Frank said, and would remember the day always as his turning point, and that petting a skunk had perhaps brought him luck.

But Eileen was looking at the sky off towards Monument. There was an odd quaver about it, as though Something was passing. As long as she lived she would think of this as the day she nearly saw an angel, and, not believing, would laugh at herself.

CHAPTER EIGHTEEN

It was the last day of school, and Lille felt reasonably satisfied. The three leaving eighth grade knew enough to get through life—they could read a book, write a brief essay, do all the functions of ordinary math. They could find themselves on a map of the country, and America on a globe of the world. They could recognize fifty famous names and tell what their owners had done. They knew American History and some World History. They could recognize birds and plants and knew what not to eat, though their parents had probably taught them that as well. They had basic manners. One of the boys was going to high school, and the other might but was inclined to start farming right away, his family perhaps behind that. The girl was already half a slave at home. Lille hoped for an end to such things in the century to come.

All of the first grade could read, Hugh in the 6th reader already. The second grade had mastered cursive. The third grade could use ink. The fourth could read history and do long division. The fifth knew its states and capitals. The sixth could be trusted to help with the younger ones and spell each other down. The seventh grade as she taught it was eighth grade Part One: if they worked at things (including Maine history) for two years, they went out in style.

Gladys was now much the cleanest one of her family and had voluntarily learned quite a lot about Africa, which for some reason she fancied. Frank had lately taken on a kind of dignity with his energy; he had told Lille that he was going to be a lawyer. She thought in fact that he'd be an excellent one, and she'd hire him. Millie Goss had shut up about religion a bit since the mysterious disappearance of the minister. On the whole, a satisfactory year, and to celebrate it she'd made a double batch of molasses donuts; they were all crazy about molasses and poured it over their bread whenever they got a chance. It was a sunny day, so they'd be eating their lunches outdoors and she'd join them, bringing the donuts.

At home, too, it was good. Her mother was up and around again, and Lib was the happiest he'd ever been, and the most confident. She could almost imagine a time when she could get away, go for a couple of weeks, say, to visit her old roommate in Bar Harbor and see the ocean again. She had enough money for the train and some new clothes. Just speculation, she wouldn't get her hopes up yet.

"Where would you like to eat your lunch?" she asked her students when noontime drew near. "Nobody's using the baseball field, or the church lawn, or the parsonage field behind us. This whole section, between one road and the other, is ours today."

The choices were nearly too much for them. Each gazed at the others and feared to speak foolishly. Then Frank showed his leadership. "Hugh," he said, "you always have good ideas. This was your first year at school. You pick."

"Brilliant!" thought Lille. She nodded.

Hugh had already been choosing in his mind. "Beside the school," he said, "but farther up the hill where we can see all the places from, and the grass is soft." Applause. Hugh inclined his head.

They settled into the tall grass like partridge babies. Lille passed out the donuts, to cries of pleasure. Devil's paintbrushes were growing in the grass beside them, daisies, short blue flowers that could be slid from their sheaths; the lucky few found wild strawberries. Two sixth-grade girls, leaning on their elbows, had begun to hum. In the midst of this tranquility, Millie Goss—it would be Millie Goss, thought Lille—stood up and shrieked on a note of satisfaction, pointing to the cemetery across the road, "The dead in Christ shall rise first!"

Indeed a kind of head-shaped gray object was slowly rising

from one of the graves. Though it didn't look like anyone else's image of the Raptured dead, the rout of the school luncheon party was picking up speed until Frank stood up and yelled, "It's only my father's shovel that I left there the other day! Sit down and eat your donuts!" In the light of that sanity the party was able to see that the head-shaped object was indeed the business end of a shovel. But why was it rising?

All over town surprises were occurring. In the Nickerson house, the True Blue Enamel chamber pot that lived under Clara's bed, a clean and humble servant, rose with dignity and drifted towards the window, where it knocked against the glass. Clara and the hired girl, whooping with laughter and surprise, throwing open the window, saw it rise solemnly into the sky and out of sight. The hired man was chasing his favorite spading fork, which was just then leaving the barn door along with a Peavey used in the annual river drive, and a bucksaw. Ducking those two slowed him down and at last, abandoned, he stood in the barnyard and cried, "Why YOU, you sonofabitch? Why? You were my favorite fork!" Later it became clear that only virtuous objects, obedient, congenial, had risen in this strange rapture. Base metal was also favored, and tools with histories—a lot of family draw-shaves went up. Nails, unless much re-used and never cursed, would not ascend; hammers well might. There would later be revelations about jewelry passed off as gold and now showing its baser nature.

Kitchens were bereaved of sieves and dippers, flour sifters, mashers and ricers, big spoons beloved of generations and cooking forks with their tines worn lopsided. Lib's oar-locks detached themselves and flew up to glory. The air was thick with sled runners and trowels, the graceful curves of scythes and sickles, hand bells and farm bells, someone's trumpet, sewing scissors. Perley would speculate later that hurtful things tended not to be included, however useful— traps or guns, cruel bits for horses' mouths. There were exceptions. Those standing near enough the lake, or facing it, saw rise up, trailing its chain and rope, the enormous hook on which Odin and his cohorts had metaphorically fixed their dreams and literally affixed the body of the first peddler. Its rising blew away the dreams, but the peddler was still visible, dark, dripping, and bloated, hanging from three of the four hooks. From the fourth hook something hung that might have been an arm, trailing a portion of what seemed to be a coat like the butt of a beetle. Something appeared to have bitten off the rest of it, if indeed it had once been larger.

The Currans, all three of them, were among the people who saw the hook rise darkly into the sky. Her parents were worried that Eileen would have nightmares, but she was a much tougher cookie than they understood. She merely hoped for a chance to tell Frank, in detail, what she'd seen.

Back at the school grounds, where the water bucket had rolled its way down the steps and headed for the clouds, objects were flying out of children's pockets like a small ascending rain: coins, pen knives, pencil stubs, cheap but cherished watches, lead soldiers and horses, safety pins, whistles, harmonicas, tin doll-dishes, whatever had fit their hands when they left the house. Who knew they had all that stuff, Lille wondered, and felt the pitch pipe escaping from her own pocket.

And the tug at her head? She threw her hands up in joy, she danced in the grass, for there flew her pesky hairpins, up and away, singing of freedom, and her hair itself, liberated, blew in a sudden wind: she felt the 20th century on her cool scalp, and she dreamed of scissors.

CHAPTER NINETEEN

The Boston Globe, Evening Edition, June 26, 1899
Your wandering correspondent made his way by train and hired
wagon to the tiny and ironically named town of Leviathan in Maine's
Aroostook County, the land of lakes and potatoes, where a remarkable
incident was said to have taken place last Friday. According to a
message conveyed to our office via Mr. Edison's invention, a number
of assorted objects took flight in Leviathan beginning at midday,
heading straight up and apparently disappearing into Heaven, perhaps
giving rise to the assertion that they were all objects of particular
virtue. Citizens to whom your reporter spoke seemed disinclined
either to testify to what they had seen or to permit their children to
speak with him, though they did not deny the event itself and
sometimes named a lost object before they locked their jaws. An
individual called Odin Crocker, more helpful than most, admitted that
an unusually large hook had emerged from the lake towards the end of
the phenomenon, but whose it might have been and what it was
designed to catch were beyond his conjecture. Nor had he any opinion
about the nature of the bait, though he speculated that it was the work
of his Canadian neighbors on the shores of East Grand's international
waters. Your correspondent regrets that Leviathan's Great Rising of
Predominantly Metal Tools must join Friar Bacon's Brazen Head and
the Loch Ness Monster in the ranks of the unaccountable.

CHAPTER TWENTY—EPILOGUE

Though the neighbors could have told Manfred's family that he was making excellent whiskey back in the woods, they thought it more polite not to. When he died in the winter of 1913 without ever having gone home to stay, he was able to leave his surviving children enough unexpected money to facilitate their dreams. Clara, who had liked this quality in Manfred, applauded.

Lille without hesitation telegraphed her old Coburn roommate: SUMMER IN EUROPE. WANT TO COME? Her roommate did. In that last enchanted summer before the guns tore it up, Lille had time to fall in love with France as she'd always known she would. She bought herself a loose summer coat that sang of Paris ever after—muted blue edged with a pattern of oriental influence. When they were old, Lille and her friend would still laugh about that summer, its freedoms and mishaps and glory, and sometimes they'd try on the coat. But pain au chocolat caused her to think fondly of her work, about the day France had been in the cemetery across the road and they'd got the spirit of it right; she came home feeling more peaceful than she ever had, her greatest itch scratched, small exotic gifts in her bags, first-hand foreign scenes in her head.

All the same she was the first woman in Leviathan to bob her hair and shorten her skirts, and the old men on the School Committee could like it or lump it. They liked it.

Lib had kept his plans to himself, as was his wont, and surprised everyone when he bought the general store, thus distancing himself from hooved animals. He loved the power of ownership. He tore off the old steps, once the site of gossip and plot, replacing them with shorter boards and less inviting treads. He expanded the hardware section at one end of the store, while in the other he put a small lending library and supplied it with a pair of kitchen chairs painted yellow. The works of Gene Stratton Porter and Zane Gray were much thumbed, but Lib made sure to save a corner for Thoreau and Emerson. After he married, another sensation, he risked a shelf of popular poetry, and built a balcony on the lake side of the storekeeper's quarters upstairs.

Lib would never tell the story of his marriage proposal to the once-dusty Gladys, only a dozen years younger than he, but Leviathan speculated that someone had taken a fit, possibly (they hoped) Ruby. Gladys, marveling at her own rise in the world—a storeowner's wife!—proved in everything the best of mates and assistants. "You can look right out at the water!" she told Lille and Clara, who, though not excited about the link to Ruby and Edna Mabel, admitted that Gladys was a gem. As soon as business allowed, Lib bought a Ford motor car. Lille contributed and had it on Sundays so she could drive to church in Houlton, where she liked especially the liturgical adroitness of the Episcopalians and the sweet reason of the Unitarians. Once or twice she took Gladys, who got over-excited.

The Smith twins were drafted and sent to France. Hugh survived and came home, where like William he enjoyed a distinguished and useful academic career. Harold, dead in France of measles, was buried in a small military cemetery outside of Paris. Hugh sometimes thought of Joab Nutter's long ago Rapture sermon. He too had awakened to find his brother flown.

Eileen grew up to become a literary scholar of some repute, much traveled and a hostess of distinction. She never married or got over her cat allergy, but she and lawyer Frank Putnam were friends all their lives.

49347715R00066

Made in the USA
Middletown, DE
19 June 2019